Lessons in lace

A gender fantasy collection

Katie Oslow

Dark Fantasy Press

Printed in the United States of America

Contents

Lets get real

Writing fiction, you always worry that people will take your words the wrong way, or fail to understand the difference between a **fantasy and a reality.**

This story is an absolute fantasy, it contains elements of non-consensual gender transformation, sexual acts, and questionable consent. Sometimes it can be fun to imagine a situation like the ones depicted here, but when you do, you should always recognize that it is in the act of play. A healthy relationship is a relationship where the humanity and value of every person is respected.

Always remember that consent is key, above all else.

Be Kind, Be safe,
Ray & Katie Oslow

Trigger Warnings: Forced Feminization, Magical body transformation, Cybernetic augmentation, Mental Reconditioning, Dub-Con

The Trial of Erinth

Beth swiped her earrings off the dresser and dropped them into her purse as she scanned the bedroom for any other incriminating evidence. She was wearing a white pencil mini skirt with a blue blouse under a white blazer with one button fastened. Satisfied that she had everything, she strode out on her 3" pumps to find Marcus standing at the apartment's kitchen island sipping coffee. He was dressed in a torn and strained t-shirt and loose sweatpants.

"You're not going out like that I hope?" Beth said as she saw him.

Marcus smiled. "Yeah, heading to the gym as soon as you leave."

"Maybe I should have made you work harder then" Beth licked her lips.

"You seemed to be at your limit" Marcus did a fake flex.

Beth laughed. "You should pull the sheets off the bed and start them in the wash so she won't notice how messed up they are. Besides, we left a wet spot."

Marcus shook his head. "In four years of marriage I have NEVER started a load of laundry. Carol would know something was up immediately! That spot will be dry long before she gets home tonight."

"I hope you're right! I know what kind of temper my sister can have." Beth lifted herself up on the island to lean across it and kiss Marcus on the lips. As she came back to earth they heard the scrape of a key in the apartment door. Beth quickly straightened out her skirt while Marcus turned his back to the door to face the coffee machine.

The door swung open to reveal Carol who stopped mid stride and surveyed the scene.

"Hey hon!" Marcus said cheerfully as he pulled down a coffee mug from the shelf, "Your sister just dropped by and I was getting her a coffee while she waited for you."

He filled the cup ⅔ and looked over at Beth. "You take cream don't you?"

"Uh, yeah....cream". Beth replied while still looking at Carol.

Carol stepped into the apartment. She wore a Black and white paisley patterned maxi dress, under an oversized tan sweater. Her long black hair hung mostly free save the front locks which were pulled behind her head and braided to keep out of her eyes. Rather than a purse, she carried a large leather attaché case which she set on the dining table "Just coffee?" She asked as she opened the leather flap and reached into the bag. "You sure you haven't had enough of my husband's cream already?" She retrieved an ornately carved wooden box and set it on the table.

"Carol!" Beth objected "That's....I just can't imagine" She sputtered.

"Baby what are you even talking about?" Marcus asked. He came out of the kitchen still holding the steaming mug.

"You deny it?" Carol asked. "You want to tell me you haven't been FUCKING MY SISTER?!" Her controlled tone erupted into screams. "FOR A WHOLE MONTH?"

"Honey please!" Marcus said. "Whatever you think you know, it's not true! I haven't touched her!"

Carol looked at Marcus, tears in her eyes, then she looked at Beth and tilted her head. "Last chance sister, did you fuck my husband?"

Beth's lip quivered. She looked down at the table. "No," She lied.

Carol nodded. "Ok." She said as she opened the lid of the box. Inside a vine pattern had been carved into the wood around a large round red jewel. Carol took a deep breath and pushed the jewel.

Beth just looked at the box and then up at Carol. She was about to ask what the point of it all was when she was startled by a high pitched shriek and the sound of a breaking mug behind her.

Beth spun to see a thin woman wearing black leggings and an undersized burgundy sports bra with the logo for "St Catherine's girls prep" stretched across her very large bust. She had dirty blond hair pulled straight back into a high ponytail. She was looking down at herself and pawing at her crotch repeating "oh God, oh God, oh God!" As she pressed her right hand with its manicured elongated nails against her flat spandex covered crotch, her left hand leapt up and cupped her left boob. "What the fuck!" She cried out.

"It's called the button of Erinth!" Carol announced.

"UNDO IT!" The woman cried.

"Who is that?" Beth asked. "Where is Marcus?"

"So you remember Marcus?" Carol asked. "Not Marcy, my wife?" She indicated the woman who was still feeling herself up.

"Marcy?" Beth asked. "No...."

"Now I know." Carol said. "The button of Erinth is an ancient magical device bound up with sexual intimacy. If my husband had never fucked you, you wouldn't remember him right now. No one out in the world does." She stepped around the table, eyes locked on Beth who walked backwards to stay out of her sister's reach.

"Help me!" Marcy cried. "My dick is gone!"

"Shut up and pay attention, wife! Unless you want to stay that way!" Carol snapped.

Marcy's eyes looked like they were about to burst into tears but she kept quiet.

"Carol, what is this?" Beth asked.

"A Forbidden item. One of the things I keep locked up under the shop for everyone's safety. It is an ancient and powerful artifact that only works within the bonds of sexual intercourse. When I suspected what was going on between you two, I dug it up." Carol explained.

Beth had backed into the wall next to the bedroom door.

Carol glanced at the disheveled sheets and saw the damp circle the lovers had left behind.

"It shifts reality" Carol moved in close and was now face to face, looking down at her slightly shorter sister. "We now live in a world where there was never a Marcus. Marcy was always a girl, and we had a lovely 2 dress wedding 4 years ago last week. I only remember otherwise because Marcus was my last sexual partner, you only remember him for the same reason."

"So pressing this button turned me into a girl?" Marcy asked.

Carol turned around to see Marcy standing triumphantly at the table, hand hovering over the red jewel. She smiled so wide it hurt her cheeks and she tried to suppress a laugh. "That's exactly what happened."

"Well then!" Marcy said with a smile and pressed the jewel. Her smile wavered as she looked down at her tits still pressed and bulging in her too small sports bra. She cupped her tits in her hands and actually tried to push them in.

Carol strode across the room and slammed the lid of the box shut.

"WHAT THE FUCK?!" Cried a man's deep voice behind her. Where Beth had been, now stood a 6' tall man with close cropped hair and a goate wearing a white suit with black loafers.

Carol looped a padlock through the latch in the box lid and scrambled the combination lock.

"Naughty girl, Marcy!" Carol said. "Didn't I tell you the button was bound up with sexual intimacy? When you press it, your last sexual partner switches sexes. The legends are unclear as to why it was made, but it works! The proof is as plain as the tits on your chest and the cock between Ben's legs".

"Carol! I can't go out like this!" Ben pleaded and then his hand went up to his throat as he heard how deep his voice had become. He stroked his chin and got a disgusted look on his face. He smoothed the front of his shirt and then his hand went down between his legs and closed. He gasped as his fingers gripped the new bulge there. His gasp sharpened as he squeezed a little too hard. "Oh fuck!" He said.

"Good idea." Carol said. "I'll consider changing you both back, if you are good and fucked first!"

"What?" Marcy squeaked in terror.

"You heard me." Carol said. "You, dear wife, are going to take my brother's cock and I am going to watch." She stepped face to face with the quivering girl and whispered in her ear "I want to see the look in your eyes the first time his dick slides up into that new pussy you have"

"Please no." Marcy whimpered.

"Then keep your pussy!" Carol said louder. "And without Marcy's help, you're stuck with that dick! I'll only let my husband use the button, not this bitch!" She said to Ben.

"No!" Ben said "Marcus please!"

"Marcy" Carol interjected. "That girl's name is Marcy".

Marcy looked at Carol for mercy but none was to be found. She looked down at her breasts, then up at Ben. Her eyes drifted to the bedroom and she grimaced. She closed her eyes, took a deep breath and said "Ok. If that's what it takes to make you happy"

Carol's eyes flared. "You think any of this will make me happy? Oh no! This isn't about happiness, or reconciliation or teaching a lesson, this is fucking revenge and it's going to take a lot more than this ONE time before I decide if I want to change you back! I literally have you both by the balls and I'm going to squeeze! You can stop at any time, but the moment you do, I fuck another man, break the link and you are stuck with tits forever!" She spun to face Ben while pointing at Marcy, "She is at my mercy and you are at hers! If YOU don't do everything I say, I'll have her fuck some random frat-boy so your link is broken too! Do the two of you understand?"

Ben and Marcy stood shaking in terror. As Carol stared into each of their eyes, they nodded.

"Good! Now get in there and get undressed while I pop some popcorn!"

In the bedroom, Marcy looked away from Ben as she fumbled, trying to reach the clasp of her sports bra, managing to get the clips parted one at a time until it finally fell open and her breasts pushed the spandex garment out in front of her. As it slid down her arms, she paused and looked down at her breasts, cupping one and tracing her large areola with her finger. She shuddered at the sensitivity. In the kitchen she could hear the whir of the Microwave intercut with a pop-pop. The bitch was really making popcorn!

She sat on the bed and bent forward to untie her sneakers. Her ponytail fell to the side of her face and the weight of her tits almost pulled her over as she leaned. She couldn't take this for long. With her shoes off she cast a glance across the bed at Ben before she hooked her thumbs under the waistband of her leggings.

Ben was still unbuttoning his shirt, it was strange doing it backwards. He pulled it off to find that he was wearing a plain v-neck white T-shirt which he pulled up over his head and tossed aside. For a moment he reached behind his back but remembered that he had no bra to unclasp, so he kicked off his shoes and unbuckled his black leather belt.

He pulled his pants and underwear down at the same time, for the first time, he saw the penis between his legs. It was soft and hung lifeless from him. He touched it gently and bit his lip to avoid crying.

Across the bed, Marcy was mourning her own loss as her fingers traced through the narrow tuft of pubic hair and probed the lips of her new labia. She slipped a finger between the lips and found the small nub of her clit, the sensitivity was surprising but the sensation was horrifying. She jerked her hand away and looked up at Ben, now naked, hairy chested with a cock that, though limp, was larger than the one Marcy had an hour a go. She shivered.

"Uh oh! Limp dick!" Carol mocked as she carried a

chair from the dining table into the bedroom and set it at the foot of the bed. "You're gonna have to bring that to life Marcy, better get to work!" She turned and left the room.

Marcy climbed up on the bed and, with a shaking hand, wrapped her fingers around Ben's penis and began to stroke,trying to replicate the way she had liked it when she had masturbated with her own dick. Ben's cock gained a little girth but still didn't get hard.

"Do you know what the secret of a good hand job is?" Carol asked as she sat in her chair with a steel popcorn bowl balanced on her lap. "Step one, use your mouth."

Marcy fought back a retch as she lifted Ben's cock to her lips and opened her mouth. It tasted bitter and a little like sweat. She closed her eyes and tried not to think about what she was doing as she flicked her tongue around the head and under the shaft the way Carol used to do. Ben' cock finally began to stiffen. When it was a solid shaft she pulled her mouth off.

""Oh my GOD! That felt so good!" Ben exclaimed.

"Lay back sweetie so my Ben can see what it's like to fuck a girl." Carol instructed.

Marcy looked back at her wife. "Please don't".

"Leave anytime, but you'll be in panties from now on." Carol said harshly.

Marcy closed her eyes and laid back with her head toward Carol.

"Eyes open girlie" Carol commanded.

Marcy opened her eyes and saw that Carol was standing over the bed now looking down on her as Ben climbed up between her legs.

"I'm sorry" Ben said and thrust. His cock hit Marcy's slit and then slid up her belly.

"First time jitters," Carol said. "Marcy, you're gonna have to guide him in."

Marcy reached down and wrapped her hand around Ben's cock. It was so large that her thumb didn't touch the fingertips. She made sure it was lined up as Ben lowered himself. She felt it push through the folds of her lips, and then it plunged in and she felt a tremendous surge of sensation, pleasure and sharp pain at the same time. Her eyes went wide, she had just had her cherry popped. As Ben started to rhythmically work his hips, she realized that she had a man's dick inside her. The feeling was insane, nothing was where it was supposed to be. Tears rolled down the sides of her face as she looked up at Carol who was grinning down at her.

In mere moments, Ben grunted and Marcy could feel him spurting inside her. "Oh God" she thought "I'm full of sperm!"

"There it is!" Said Carol's mocking voice. "The moment you truly understand what it is to be fucked!" She bent down and kissed Marcy on the forehead.

Marcy felt Ben slide out of her and then a trickle of liquid ran down her ass. Another wet spot.

"I want to see this at least eight more times in

the next month, raw dog, with creampies," Carol announced. "In thirty days, if I'm satisfied, I'll press the button. As long as you're not pregnant, it should swap you back."

Marcy looked up at Ben in sheer terror as she felt his cum running down her backside. "Pregnant?" she gasped.

"Yup, The button of Erinth will never take a mother from a child. You get knocked up, it's permanent, and I'm banning condoms. Good luck with that!" Carol said as she walked out the door slamming it behind her.

—

Thirty days later, Marcy sat at the Dining room table. She was wearing a black and red low-cut minidress. Carol had forbidden her to wear anything masculine or modest all month. Ben sat beside her in Jeans and a T-shirt. The two held hands as they watched Carol fish the box out of her bag.

"You sure you don't want to go one last round before I press," Carol mocked. "I noticed that Ben is hard from the beginning these days and, Marcy, you try to hide it, but I know you've climaxed with Ben inside you at least twice now."

"Just push the button!" Marcy grumbled as she felt her cheeks flush in embarrassment. The truth was that she had orgasmed every time for the past two weeks.

"Watch that tone or it's another month in skirts, Missy" Carol admonished.

"Sorry mistress" Marcy lowered her head.

"And we are keeping that attitude even when you have a dick, or I'm taking it away again!" Carol said.

"Yes mistress." Marcy was utterly defeated. Even when returned to manhood, she would forever be the submissive slave of her wife.

Carol opened the lid of the box. "Now that we're clear." She said as she pushed down on the jewel and.....nothing happened.

Marcy looked at the box in astonishment.

Ben jerked his hand away and uttered "Oh God NO!"

Marcy's heart thundered and she grew queasy in recognition of what this meant.

"Well!" Carol said. "Congratulations Mommy!"

Hailey's Lessons

1, Henry's Punishment

"It's not true Dad." Henry said weakly as he turned and walked shakily toward the garage.

His Dad said nothing. When Henry looked over his shoulder he saw his Dad leaning against the hallway wall staring at the ceiling and crying. It was the most painful thing he had ever seen.

The Garage door was open and the luxury SUV's motor was running when Henry got to the Garage.

"There you are," His mother said. "Buckle up please."

"Mom, I don't have my wallet and Dad broke my phone," Henry said.

"NO!" she answered sharply. She paused, took a breath and explained. "You won't be needing either of those. Everything is ready for you." She said as she backed the SUV into the turn-around and then drove out through the gates.

"Ready?" What do you mean?" Henry asked.

His mom took a deep breath. "Your father and I believe you need a new perspective. You are going to live with someone who specializes in providing that."

Henry's breath quickened "But school! I have Senior exams coming! Prom!"

"You can still finish, We are not sending you far away." She said,

Henry relaxed a little. No matter what kind of disciplinary bullshit awaited him where they were going, he would at least have a few hours of normalcy and, more importantly, more chances to get Wendy to tell the truth.

"I didn't do that to Monica!" Henry said after they had driven a few miles in silence. He saw his mother's hands tighten on the wheel.

"Were you having sex?" She asked.

"Mom!" Henry said in shock.

"You were!" She said flatly. "And if she got into trouble, what would you have done?"

"Mom! I didn't!" Henry whined.

"I don't know that!" She snapped. "It doesn't matter anyway! You need to learn that girls are not play-things young man!"

"I don't! Wendy was lying!" Henry started.

"Spare me!" His mom cut him off. She turned and drove through another set of gates up a curved driveway to a house that was only a little smaller than Henry's and came to a stop in front of the door. She turned to Henry. "The woman who lives here is Miss Molly Greenfield. You will call her Ma'am or Miss at all times! You will obey her instructions and you will not talk back! Is that understood?"

"I don't have to do this!" Henry replied defiantly. "I'm 18, I can go where I want!"

"Not to school. We pay your tuition to Ovid

Academy and we are paying your tuition to University in the fall! You think you can make it out there on your own? Finish up at a public school? Flip burgers to barely cover rent? You never worked a day in your life! By all means, it would be as good a lesson as Miss Greenfield could teach! Choose now! Walk out into the street or up to that door! Either way, YOU will deal with the consequences of your choice for once!"

She reached across the car and opened Henry's door. "We are done."

Henry cast a pleading tearful look at his mother but her expression was stern and she said nothing. Finally, dreading the heavy silence, he stepped out of the SUV. He looked down the long driveway to the open gate. If he left, where would he go? All his friends lived with their parents and after the rumor Wendy had started, none of them would want Henry around. His heart pounding, he turned toward the large green door and began up the stairs of the ornate porch. Behind him he could hear his mother's luxury SUV drive away.

The door swung open before he could press the bell. Henry had expected a stern old woman, but Miss Greenfield looked like she was in her early 30s at most. She had brown hair, an athletic figure and stood several inches taller than Henry. "Ohh, you're a little one!" She exclaimed. "That should make this go smoother!"

Henry swallowed his pride and indignation. The only way past this was through. He would do what was expected without complaint and prove to his parents that he was not the person Wendy had said he was. "Good evening Miss Greenfield. My name is Henry. My mother said that I will be staying with you for a while. May I come in?"

Miss Greenfield smiled. "What lovely manners! Come on, Little one!" She stepped aside to allow Henry into the large foyer. To his left he saw a formal dining room. To his right was a parlor filled with antique furniture. A staircase climbed up the right wall, to a second floor. It was a nice place, but it smelled a little musty and dust could be seen accumulated on the cherry wood table against the wall.

"I apologize for the condition of the house!" She said, "I have just taken over as caretaker and my predecessor seemingly neglected the basics."

"It's fine," Henry replied.

"It will be. With your help!" She said,

"Yes ma'am" After his mother's tirade, he had expected to be doing work.

"But first! Let's get you settled. Follow me!" Miss Greenfield beckoned Henry up the stairs.

He followed her to the top and through a pair of double doors into a massive room with a canopy bed draped in pink linens set in the center of the far wall. An antique vanity with an oval mirror sat by the door, a jewelry case on one side and a makeup kit on the other.

"This will be your room!" Miss Greenfield said.

"Oh?" Henry gasped. The makeup was all laid out

and he could see fresh wrappers in the garbage can. He had assumed this was Miss Greenfield's room.

"Oh?" she repeated, her brow bunched up. "I believe you intended to say 'yes ma'am"

Henry gulped. "Yes ma'am!"

She smiled wide. "Good! Now take off your clothes!"

"Ma'am?" Henry was stunned.

She cleared her throat. "You can leave at any time!"

Henry remembered the long driveway to the unknown. He pulled off his shirt while Miss Greenfield stood and watched. He dropped his pants to the ground and stood in his boxers.

"A Job half done is not a job worth doing!" Miss Greenfield motioned to his shorts with her eyes. "Let's see the little thing that has caused all this trouble!"

Henry gulped. Stripping in front of an attractive woman had been a little arousing. As he dropped his underwear, his penis rose to half-mast.

"Not so little I see." Miss Greenfield said. She sighed. "Seeing as that thing has got you into so much trouble, I think it best that you get it under control." She reached into her bag and pulled out a small curved metal cylinder with a ring behind it. She looked at it and then at Henry's cock. The attention and embarrassment caused him to go soft and shrink under her gaze. "Good!" She announced and dropped the device back into her bag, pulling out one that was a very short curved tube with a flat cap above the ring as she stepped forward.

Henry stepped back.

"Hold still, little one!" She demanded and came forward once more. She grabbed him by the cock and balls. He yelped and she squeezed. "I said hold still!"

Henry didn't know what to do. This strange woman was doing something with the short metal tube and ring. Squishing his soft penis into the round cap and swinging the open ring up around his balls for it to click closed with the cap. She then took a small padlock, closed it through the connecting rings and let it fall.

Henry looked down to see his penis encased in the tiny curved tube above where the ring around his balls were anchoring the whole thing in place.

"WHAT THE FUCK!" He cried.

"Language little one!" She chided. "It will come off after you have had your lesson!"

"It's crushing me!" he moaned. He pulled at it, but his balls were too big to fit through the ring and he almost fell over from the pain.

"STOP THIS INSTANT!" Miss Greenfield's voice was stern and commanding.

Henry snapped up and looked at her.

"Your mother has told me why you are here! That stays on for your own protection! Clearly managing it is beyond your capabilities! It may be uncomfortable at times, but it will teach you to keep your mind pure." She said sternly. She picked

up Henry's clothes and headed for the door. "Get some sleep, I will be waking you early tomorrow!"
"I didn't bring anything to sleep in!" Henry said.
She sighed "There are night-gowns in the wardrobe."
"Nightgowns?" Henry said indignantly.
"Put one on and go to bed or I will lose this key!" She demanded.
Henry was about to protest again but saw the fire in her eyes. "Yes Ma'am" he said at last.
She stood and watched him open the wardrobe and stare dumbfounded at the slips of cloth hanging there.
"The one on the far right" She instructed.
Henry pulled it down. It was pink and sleeveless with white lace stitching around the low cut v neck. When he pulled it on, the skirt fell only to his knees. He blushed as he turned to Miss Greenfield who only smiled.
"Wait!" Henry said. "How will I get this off when I go to the bathroom?"
She shook her head. "It has a hole, you will just have to lift your skirt and sit down like a girl, now get in bed!"
He looked for mercy in her expression and found none so he climbed in, feeling the skirt bunch up under him as he lay down.
Miss Greenfield flicked the light switch off and left the room. Henry could hear the click as she locked the door from the outside.
It was spring and daylight still streamed across the

room from the window.
Henry thought about what he would say to Wendy to get her to come clean about her story in the morning.

The click of the lock woke Henry in time to see a bright yellow light stream in from the hall. It was still dark outside. Miss Greenfield stood there with a smile "It's 5am little one! Time to rise and shine!" Henry brought his hand up to shield his eyes. "FIVE?" He asked indignantly.
"We have a new routine, you have to get ready, do chores and eat breakfast before school!" She flicked the light switch illuminating the room. "We have a lot of work to do!" She swung the chair by the vanity around to face the bed. "First thing we need to manage is that hair!"
Henry had a feeling this was coming. Over the past year and a half he had avoided trips to the barber, at first due to laziness and then because he liked the roguish look his mane of long blond hair gave him. His parents always grumbled about it and he was sure it was coming off now.
He was wrong. As soon as he sat, Miss Greenfield swept a drape over his shoulders and went to work, not hacking it off but carefully trimming the ends, adjusting the fall, and finally, she swept it over his face then expertly clipped along his brow line.
When she finished and pulled off the drape, Henry turned to inspect her work. He was in shock! He still had long flowing blond hair but now with

bangs! Sitting there in the pink nightgown, the haircut made him look like a girl. “What? What did you do?” He teased at his bangs with his fingers trying to part them or hide them somehow.

“Hair can be cut again later, little one!” she said. Now it’s time to get dressed for school!”

Henry turned and his heart dropped. Miss Greenfield had pulled a peach colored dress with a white ruffled collar and bell sleeves out of the closet and was laying it on the bed.

“I can’t wear that!” Henry exclaimed.

“It’s well within your school’s dress code.” She replied. “Dresses or Skirts mid thigh or longer, no halters or midriffs, no underwear on display.”

“That’s the girl’s dress code!” Henry exclaimed.

“Perhaps, but It is illegal for the school to discriminate based on sex.” She replied.

“I’m not a girl!” Henry went on.

“Turn around!” Miss Greenfield demanded.

“What?” Henry was confused.

“Look in the mirror!” Her tone was growing harsh.

Henry turned and looked at himself. Long blond hair with pretty bangs, in a pink frilly nightgown.

“Do you look like a boy right now?” She asked.

Henry was furious, he stood up and spun around, spinning the skirt of his nightgown as he did so. “You did this to me!”

“SIT DOWN LITTLE ONE!” Miss Greenfield shouted.

Henry stood there looking defiant.

She pulled on the chain around her neck and

displayed the key to his cage. "Sit down!"

"Give me that!" Henry demanded.

She pulled it free and handed it to him. "Ok, fine. Take off the cage and leave. You'll be on your own out there. No fancy schools or warm beds, no Mommy or Daddy to help you. Just you, all pretty in your nightgown and bangs alone in the world."

"My clothes" He started.

"Were incinerated last night!" Miss Greenfield cut him off. "Search the house, you won't find one pair of trousers. It's skirts, dresses and gowns or nothing now"

"You can't!" Henry pleaded.

"I already have, little one. I follow through when I start something. Question is, do you?" She held her hand out palm open. "Give me back the key and finish your lesson, or give up everything."

Henry could feel the trap closing on him as tight as the cage around his cock. He wanted to be brave, take a stand, set out and prove that he could make it on his own but the idea of walking down that driveway in a pink nightgown and having no idea what to do next overwhelmed him. He closed his eyes and felt a tear running down his cheek. This was going to be humiliating but he had no other choice. He put the key back in Miss Greenfield's hand.

"Good, Henry!" She replied. She quickly latched the chain around her neck once more and began pulling open drawers. "As to the dress code, yes, you will be complying with the girls dress code for the foreseeable future. Ovid Academy is an old school with rules and traditions that go back to the time when petticoating was a common disciplinary action." She pulled a pair of frilly painties out of a drawer and handed them to Henry. "Pull those on."

Henry winced as he pulled the garment up and was surprised how tight and firm it felt. Despite the rigidity of the small cage he wore there was hardly any bulge visible.

"Those will help you maintain a 'soft tuck'" She said as she approached him with a white lacy bra in her hands. "Gown off!"

Henry complied and then stood rigid while she slid the bra straps up his arms and fastened it behind his back while she talked. "The school administration is aware of your punishment and will be treating you as a girl through its duration." She went back to the same drawer she had retrieved the bra from and came back with a pair of silicone false breasts. She peeled off the plastic cover revealing the adhesive then expertly pushed them into place, letting the bra hold them to set while she adjusted his shoulder straps until the breast forms pushed his chest muscle together to emulate the swell and cleavage of real breasts. She stepped back to inspect her work and then turned back to the drawers while she talked.

"They will still call you Henry, but you will use She/Her pronouns. You will also attend gym, and use the ladies locker room and restrooms. School policy requires you to wear that cage as a result, though I find it a useful teaching tool anyway." She handed him a pair of white pantyhose.

In shock Henry just sat and began figuring out how to pull them on. They were silky, tight, and yet he could still feel a breeze on his legs. "She/her?" he repeated in disbelief.

"Yes." Miss Greenfield said. "As of right now, regardless of what is locked in your panties, you are a girl. Fail to behave in a ladylike fashion, either in language, action or dress and your time with me will be extended."

"I'm a girl?" Henry looked in the mirror, staring back at him, in a bra, panties, and hose was a girl. "I'm a girl." he said in disbelief.

"Yes Miss Henry, you are a girl for the rest of this semester and you better act like it. There is a reward for any faculty or student who can prove that you have engaged in unladylike behavior!" Miss Greenfield said as she held up the dress she had selected.

"The rest of the semester?" Henry repeated in shock.

"Longer if you don't behave!" Miss Greenfield elaborated.

Henry was in shock. "But..Prom!"

"I am sure that I can find a young man to escort you." She replied.

"NO!" Henry snapped. "I'm not gay!"

"No you are not, Miss Henry." Miss Greenfield agreed. "You are a young lady in her senior year and a proper young lady is escorted to her prom by a gentleman."

"That's not what I mean!" Henry whined.

"NO!" Miss Greenfield said sternly. "It is what I demand! Now put your dress on young lady or you will be late for school!"

As Henry slipped it over his head he was mortified. He was going to school as a girl, all his friends, all the girls were going to see him mincing from class to class in a pretty dress with fake breasts! Worse than that, rather than fading into the background, EVERYONE would be watching him every day all day just waiting for him to mess up!

He wanted to plead for mercy but the words wouldn't come.

"Oh, lovely already, but let's add a little makeup!" Miss Greenfield said.

When she arrived at school, Every step Henry took in her mary-janes felt like it was in thick mud. She could feel a thousand pairs of eyes on her as she exited Miss Greenfield's car and made her way to the open door of the school.

Out of the corner of her eye, she could see Becky Shoot and her circle of friends whispering at each other. They pulled out their phones and began to record. Henry looked away.

By the entrance Henry was heading for, Robert Crow had his phone out too and a cruel smile. "Nice dress Henry!" He sneered as she passed.

Henry wanted to fight back. Robert was standing

wide legged, a single kick could ruin his day, but it wouldn't be lady-like! Instead she looked down and quicked her pace past him.

Like a wave, the hallway would grow silent as she approached, everyone looking at her. As soon as she passed, whispers and murmurs would be passed back and forth.

By the time Henry reached the library, her cheeks were on fire and she could feel tears running down her face.

Wendy was whispering happily with her friends but the table grew silent when Henry approached.

"Wendy! I need to talk to you!" Henry pleaded.

Wendy tossed her red hair, and said "Fine" before she stood and motioned to an empty table nearby.

Henry sat across from her and leaned forward, but the breast forms in her bra were in the way and the bundled flesh on her chest squished up into cleavage so severe that Wendy's eyes went wide. Henry quickly sat back up and adjusted the top of her dress to a more modest position. "You have to tell the truth!" She pleaded with Wendy. "Tell your parents that I didn't pressure Monica into getting an abortion! Tell them you just didn't want them playing matchmaker with us! PLEASE!"

Wendy sighed. "If I did that, they would still want us to get together!"

"Look at me!" Henry pleaded.

"You are a very cute girl, quite well endowed!" Wendy smirked.

"Fuck that!" Henry exclaimed.

Wendy raised an eyebrow.

Henry was furious "My fucking dick is smashed! I have to sit to fucking pee and that bitch is going to keep me like this till the end of the year! She even says she'll get a guy to take me to prom! I'm not fucking gay!" He could see Wendy looking around the room and knew he was losing his case. "Wendy please, we have been friends since we were six! Don't do this to me! So our parents would make us go out, is that so fucking awful?"

Wendy steeled her expression. "Before today? Maybe not. Now? Like I'd ever be seen on a date with Henry the girly boy!"

Henry sat back in shock like she had been slapped.

"Anyway, sweetie. Wendy spun her finger around.

Henry looked to see a dozen students and a librarian all holding their cameras pointed at her.

Wendy stood up. "Five F-bombs, dick talk and a slur? You may not be gay, but you are a nasty girl"

Henry could hear the pings of messages being sent all around the room.

Wendy smiled. "And you're going to be a girl for a very, very long time."

2, Henry's First Day

Henry looked up at Wendy in helpless shock. She felt her throat contract and her lip quiver. There was a 'Bing' from a nearby phone.

"20 bucks! YES! I got the bountie!" a boy announced to the others.

Another 'Bing'

"Me too!" said a girl behind Henry

Henry heard two more chimes and someone called out "Easy money! Thanks sissy!"

The room erupted in laughter.

Henry leapt to her feet, she felt like she was going to throw up. She had to get out of there!

She spun for the door, her skirt twirling up as she did so.

"Panty flash has got to be worth something!" someone said.

"I missed it!" came a reply

"I didn't! Very pretty Miss Henry!" said one of the librarians followed by the 'Ding' of a sent message. Henry could taste bile in her mouth. She raced out of the library as laughter followed her into a hallway where a passing freshmen looked at hier, looked away and then looked back in shock. Henry pushed past the kid into the washroom, past the urinals and into a stall.

The floor was filthy and Henry knew she would be in trouble for fouling her white pantyhose, so she braced her arms on the stall sides and bent over heaving.

She managed to keep from throwing up and calm herself. A moment's peace was enough. She realized that she had to pee, so she stood up, lifted her skirt, pulled down the front of her hose and panties and then her fingers struck the small cage her penis was encased in. It squished her almost flat, there was no way to aim it.

Resigned, Henry pulled down her frilly undergarments, turned and sat to pee. As she did so, she heard a door open and someone walk in and start to use the urinal.

Suddenly Henry realized her mistake. Under the "petticoat protocol" Henry was officially a girl at Ovid-Academy. A girl in the boys bathroom would be in a lot of trouble. She sucked in on her lips and lifted his black patent leather mary-jane shoes and stocking legs off the floor, hopefully out of sight.

She heard the flush of the urinal and the sound of the sink as whoever washed their hands.

Henry was holding her breath so as to not make a sound.

The door never opened though and Henry could hear the creak of someone leaning against the counter.

"I'm not going anywhere sissy, so you may as well come on out." It was the voice of Robert Crow.

Henry clenched her eyes and tears flowed out. She sniffed and stood. A drip of pee was hanging from her cage, she snatched a square of paper and dabbed herself, thinking how girly it was to not just shake it off. She pulled up her frilly panties, her hose, smoothed her skirt down the front, took a deep breath and opened the stall door.

Robert was holding his phone ready when the door opened and Henry heard the click as he snapped a picture. "Wrong washroom Miss Henry!" Robert said. "That's certainly worth a pretty penny to Miss Greenfield!"

"Please don't!" Henry pleaded. "Every time she gets one of those pictures, she is going to make me be a girl longer!"

"Oh, that's even more reason to send it! After all, you are so pretty right now. You should stay this way." He snapped a second picture. "That's for the spank-bank later!"

Henry was taken aback, did she look that girly, or ...."Are you gay?" She asked flatly.

"Sissy! You look like a girl, dress like a girl and everyone has to call you a girl. Nothing gay about what I'm feeling right now!" Robert sneered.

Henry shrunk back toward the stall. "Please, just leave me alone."

"Sure, I'll just hit send and collect my cash!" Robert looked down at his phone as he turned toward the door.

"NO!" Henry pleaded. "Don't send that!"

Rob stopped, his smile was ear to ear. "I won't, if

you give me a kiss!"

Henry's head spun. A boy wanted to kiss her, it was unthinkable. Then she looked at Robert's phone and wondered how much more time that photo was going to cost her. A kiss was only a moment, just the two of them, no one would know.

"Ok!" she said. "Just a kiss"

Robert set his phone down and moved in on Henry, backing her into the stall. He put a hand on the back of Henry's head. Henry was shorter than Robert. He tilted her face up to meet gis, then planted his lips on Henry's

Henry, expecting a peck was taken back, especially when Robert's tongue pushed into her mouth. Henry's eyes went wide but Robert's arms around her held her there, then Henry felt Robert's hand on her ass, gripping and squeezing through her skirt.

Henry whimpered as Robert's hand traced around his leg and then to his crotch where it closed on her caged cock.

"Nice and tight" He said as he lifted his head away.

Henry smacked her hand away and stepped back against the toilet.

"You're as good as dickless, like a girl too!" Rob smiled as he wiped a finger under his lips. "That was nice, sissy. Thanks"

He picked up his phone from the counter and walked out.

Henry starred in the mirror stunned. Her lipstick was smudged, she had seen it smeared on Robert's mouth. She needed to touch it up. Worse than that was that she suspected that Robert had recorded the whole thing.

Henry took the time to fix her lipstick rather than face rumors or the possibility of being ruled "Unladylike " then walked out of the men's washroom face to face with an older Math teacher who sternly announced. "Wrong washroom young lady! I'm putting you on report!"

Henry had let Robert Crow feel her up for nothing!

The morning bell rang and Henry had no option but to duck immediately into her home room. Mrs. Malcom Smiled at Henry as she entered and motioned for her to come in.

"Class" she called, and the chatter of gossiping teens closed out as every eye fixed on Henry. "Class, Henry is undergoing what is called a petticoating period. During this time you will refer to Henry with She/Her pronouns." She paused to let it sink in. Henry's cheeks were flush. "She is to be treated like every other girl here at Ovid Academy. With respect!"

Several of the students in the room smirked, but Henry could see others nodding in sympathy or empathy. Wendy was in the back corner watching Henry with sad eyes.

Mrs. Malcolm continued. "Also, this is a safe space for Henry! Where she should be allowed to explore her girlhood without fear. So, there will be no collection of bounties in this room!" Henry sighed in relief. The moment of peace she needed! Mrs.

Malcom turned to Henry then. “However, if I find that you are openly defying the terms of Petticoating, I will withdraw that protection. Is that clear, young lady?”

Henry nodded. “Yes ma’am, Thank you ma’am”

Ms. Malcolm nodded. “You may take a seat!”

Henry went back to the open desk beside Wendy. She had to get her to change her mind.She swung around the chair as always, and sat down.

“Stop!” Wendy said.

Henry raised an eyebrow.

“Stand back up!” She demanded.

“No,” Henry demanded.

“Do you want to keep getting flagged or do you want to learn how to be a girl so you can stop being a girl someday?” She asked.

Henry sighed and stood back up.

“You went to the toilet, didn’t you?” She asked.

“How did..” He began

“You didn’t get your panty hose all the way up, there is a gap between the gusset and your panties.” Wendy said.

“What’s a gusset?”

“The fabric part in the middle, now pull up the legs and then fix your hose!” Wendy demanded.

“Here?” Henry balked.

“Mrs. Malcolm?” Wendy called. “Can I take Henry to the ladies room so I can show her how to fix herself up?”

“That’s very kind of you Wendy! I’m sure Henry will be grateful.” Mrs. Malcolm held out her hall pass.

The girls bathroom had pink tile rather than the mint-green of the boy's room. Henry was surprised to see paper towels and toilet tissue on the floor. It wasn't nearly as neat and clean as she had expected.

Wendy lifted Henry's skirt and pointed out where to pull to get her hose all the way up her legs. She then handed her a makeup cleansing wipe. "We are going to have to redo the whole face!" She said, "Seems Miss Greenfield didn't give you waterproof and you have been crying!"

"Waterproof?" Henry was irritated that it was an option that had not been offered.

"You are going to be doing this for a while, so you need to learn. I'll do it this time, but next time it's you!" She announced.

Henry turned her back to the mirror and let Wendy get to work. She was happy not to have to see herself like this.

"I'm sorry Henry." She said sadly.

"This is your fault," Henry said. It wasn't a tone of accusation, more disbelief. "You can fix this."

"It's too late now!" Wendy insisted. "The lie has grown too big. If I come clean now, after putting you through all this, I don't know what they will do to me."

"Look at what they are doing to me!" Henry pleaded.

"That's what I mean!" She snapped. "I can't take this! Now look up!"

Henry did so as Wendy lined her under eye, drawing it out past the corner and up. "Look down" She drew a line from where she stopped back to Henry's eyelid and colored in the gap, then did the same with his right eye. As she colored in the last bits she broke her silence.

"If they are doing this to you, what they do to me will be much worse. I'm sorry Henry, but I'm not strong enough to face that. I think you are!" She said with shame in her voice. She closed her eyeliner and picked up an eyelash wand.

Henry grabbed her by the wrist. "Shouldn't I get to decide if I'm strong enough?"

Wendy looked Henry in the eye for a long time then finally said. "If I was a better person, yes."

Henry dropped her hand. Wandy wasn't cruel, she was scared, and Henry had no way to push through her fear. The argument was lost. She held still and let her finish her eyes.

Wendy applied some blush too and then packed everything back in her purse. "You will need a makeup kit of your own." She said, "I'll bring you one tomorrow."

"Do you have a hair tie?" Henry asked. The constant embarrassment was making him hot so he had decided to tie her hair back in a ponytail.

"Sit in front of me when we get back, I'll fix your hair." she replied.

"Thanks" Henry said glumly as they made their way back to class.

In Mrs. Malcolm's home room, Henry could feel

Wendy behind him pulling and twisting her hair. "Girls," Wendy said loud enough to be heard by her friends. "Henry is going to be a girl for the rest of the term. I think she should sit with us at lunch."
The girls looked at each other. Becky Simpson curled her nose. "Sissy boy?"
"You heard Mrs. Malcom. We are treating her with respect!" Wendy snapped back. "The same respect that keeps people from calling you CumDump"
Becky went red but the other girls laughed.
"Fine!" Becky said to save face "She can sit with us! I was just giving her a hard time!"
"Good! Aaaaaan DONE" Wendy said and let go of Henry's hair.
As she sat up, he didn't feel the mane on his shoulders, rather a cord seemed to land on her back. She reached back and felt the braid. Pulling it around she found a pink bow neatly tied to its end. She resisted the urge to pull it off.
"That's a very pretty bow Henry," Mrs. Malcolm said from the front of the class.
Henry dropped it. Everyone was looking at her again. "Thank you," she said.
Mrs. Malcolm smiled and went back to her reading.
The next classes were instruction heavy, sparing Henry too much shame as everyone was focused on preparing for exams.
At lunch she sat with Wendy and the other girls, shyly listening to them gossip about each other and talk about boys. There was a rumor circulating around that Robert Crow couldn't get

it up for Sheryl Leaf at a party last week. Henry thought that she knew why but she kept it to herself wanting to forget the encounter in the boys room as much as possible.

For Gym class Henry stood frozen in the hallway to the changing rooms, afraid to go in until Mrs. Paula the PE teacher came over to him.

"Same as washrooms Miss Henry!" She said,

"But, the other girls!" She was worried they may think she was a creep spying on them.

"They all know you're locked down and harmless! Mrs. Paula announced. "There's a girl's uniform waiting for you in locker 22.

Sure enough, a pair of short shorts, a sports bra and a form fitting ladies T shirt with the school logo was in locker 22 and fit Henry perfectly. As she pulled down her hose, exposing his frilly panties, she heard some whispers and giggles behind her, but no one said a word.

On the field, Wendy coaxed Henry into the circle of girls who walked and chatted rather than run laps. The first time the Boys ran past them, Robert Crow yelled "Sissy!"

The second time, she was joined by a few others.

By the time class was over, the boys were cheering "Sissy Henry! Sissy Henry!" Every time they went by.

The chant took off around the school so that when Henry walked into her last period class, the boys in the room all gave it three repetitions before Mr. Pinehurst banged on the table to shut them up.

At school pickup, outside the library, Henry stood with Wendy and heard every time a Boy would shout "Sissy Henry" while laughing with his friends. The feeling of wanting to vomit had not left her all day and she was relieved when Miss. Greenfield pulled up in her Red sports car.
"I like the eyeliner wings Henry!" Miss Greenfield said as soon as he climbed into the car.
Henry just nodded.
"A proper lady would have said thank you!" Miss Greenfield said as she pulled away. "You have made quite a display of yourself today!"
"I know." Henry said, sick to her stomach. "I'm sorry"
"I had a call with your parents while I was waiting for pickup Henry." She said as she drove down the narrow lane toward the house. "After this morning, we think it best that your corrective period continues through the summer."
Henry gasped and turned. Miss Greenfield snapped a quick look back at him. There was no negotiation in her eyes. "This way, you will be properly prepared to behave yourself when you start college in the fall."
"All summer, Ma'am?" Henry asked sheepishly. Vacation plans dissolved in her mind.
"All summer!" She replied. "Though your parents do want you with them on the cruise ship"
Henry cracked a small smile.
"You will, of course, be attending as their daughter." Miss Greenfield added. "And the key

stays here with me"

Henry's relief was replaced with new horror at the prospect of wearing a girl's swimsuit on foreign beaches. Tears welled in Henry's eyes. "Yes, ma'am," she replied.

They were pulling up the drive to the house.

"Now, you have chores little Miss." Miss Greenfield said as she parked. "Your uniform and list of tasks are waiting on your bed. This will be your routine on afternoons and weekends while you are with me."

"Yes ma'am" Henry said defeatedly. Her mind still stuck on the fact that he would spend his entire summer break as a girl.

She trudged upstairs to her room.

Laid out on her bed was a black and white french maid uniform with a short puffy skirt. On the floor in front of it were a pair of black 3" narrow heels. She dropped the pink book bag she had carried all day and shook her head.

"Of course." she said as she ran her finger along the silky shimmery finish of the black fabric. "What else?"

Henry was extremely unsteady in the heels as she tottered out of her room, the ruffled petticoats under her skirt and silicone inserts bouncing with every step.

"Ladies glide Miss. Henry! Tramps bounce!" Miss Greenfield chided her as she emerged into the hallway. "Go slow, walk heel-toe, one foot in front of the other, small steps!" she instructed.

Henry shifted her stride and while she still felt wobbly, she was much smoother, though frustratingly slow as she carried the task list to the pantry and retrieved a feather duster, a rag and a can of furniture polish. She had decided to work top to bottom, starting with the crown molding, then the walls and furniture and finishing up by vacuuming the carpet and polishing the hard wood.

Click-tap glide, click-tap glide, she made her way to the entry and got started.

When the doorbell rang, Henry was in the Library, on a footstool dusting the top of the shelves.

"I'll get it Henry!" Miss Greenfield called.

Nodding, Henry continued with her task. She did not hear anyone come in until she heard a familiar voice say "Nice view!"

Henry froze, realizing that how she was positioned, anyone in the Library doorway would be able to see her frilly panties right up her skirt. She stepped back, stomach churning to see Robert Crow leering at her and licking his lips.

Miss Greenfiedl walked in and out an arm around him.

"Henry, This morning you told me how worried you were about missing prom!" She grinned.

"Oh no." Henry said to herself

"Robert here has agreed to be your escort!" Miss Greenfield said beaming! "Oooh I can't wait to get you into the perfect little Prom dress! You and Robert will make such a lovely couple!"

Henry was frozen in shock.

“I’m looking forward to it!” Robert said. He looked Henry in the eyes. “I’m sure it's going to be an amazing night for both of us!”

3, Henry's Prom night

The Black and white maid dress with its frilly trim was hanging right in front of the open door to Henry's closet. Her eyes moved across the lace and satin finish, and for once, she wished she was wearing it. She let out a wistful sigh and as she exhaled Miss Greenfield pulled the ribbon laces tight on the corset dress she was helping Henry get into. As the waist cincher, Henry felt a moment of panic. She tried to gasp but could only pull in a little air before she hit the limits of the garment.
"Ma'am, I can't breathe!" She complained.
"The fact that you can whine about it tells me you can, little one!" She said unsympathetically as she tied the laces into a double knot before stuffing the ends up under the bottom of the corset leaving the large dark green ribbon bow as a decoration on Henry's back. She took Henry by the shoulders and turned her to face the full length mirror.
The dress was forest green with spaghetti straps. The corset was covered in shiny green panels with gold flower embroidery. The bust was covered in green sequins that shimmered in the light. Underneath, medical tape and silicone inserts pushed Henry's pecks together giving

the appearance of swelling cleavage beneath the sweetheart neckline. The A-line skirt was made of glittering tulle and had a double slit so that Henry's black thigh-high fishnets were on display with every step she made in her gold 3" stiletto heels. The green and gold of the dress matched the emerald and gold necklace, rings and bracelets she wore as well as the long pendants hooked into her newly pierced ears.

Her hair had been professionally styled into a feminine up-do with curled strands framing her face which had also been professionally made over at the salon earlier in the day despite her pleading to let Wendy come do it in the house.

The women at the salon had too much fun gathering around and commenting about the "brave trans girl" getting her hair done. Henry knew they were trying to be supportive, but she was humiliated that they thought this was what she wanted. Ms. Greenfield had, of course, forbidden her from correcting the ladies, so Henry spent the morning being told how pretty she was and how her prom date would be so turned on he wouldn't be able to think straight.

Now, Henry had to admit that they were right. The girl looking back at Henry in the mirror was beautiful! Nothing of the boy showed through at all. By now, It had been weeks since Henry had been allowed to be a boy. Blouses and skirts at school, maid uniforms for chores and a sundress when she went to the park with Wendy. Henry was starting to wonder what was left of the boy they locked away inside herself. Would she remember how to be a boy when the summer ended and she could be herself once more?

She suddenly realized that, in her own internal monologue, she was using feminine pronouns. Was the boy truly gone?

"Robert is going to be over the moon when he sees you!" Miss Greenfield beamed over Henry's shoulder as she adjusted one of the dangling strands by her face. "Boys will be boys after all and this is Prom night!"

"If he touches me, I'll deck him!" Henry grumbled.

Miss. Greenfield's eyes flashed. "You will do no such thing! A lady must not resort to violence. You must find other ways to preserve your virtue!"

"How?" Henry pleaded.

Miss. Greenfield sighed. "Appeal to his good nature. From what I have seen of Robert, If you set a proper and chaste example, he will not be tempted."

"And if he is?" Henry interjected.

"Then you must have done something to encourage him. Most unladylike!" She replied. "Now, Wait up here till he arrives. Your Mother will call you down. She wants a full set of staircase photos and then a few by the fireplace before you head out."

"My mother is here?" Henry tried to take a deep breath but was prevented by the corset. She had not seen her since she was dropped off last month. Since then, the only time Henry heard from her was when Miss Greenfield relayed a new punishment to correct Henry for not acting "Girly Enough." The ear piercings, the manicure, the eyebrow pluck and today's visit to the salon had all come about that way. "What about my Dad?"

Miss Greenfield shook her head. "I am under the impression that he has stepped aside where you are concerned"

Henry felt her stomach lurch. His father had given up and left her to these sadistic women to be feminized. After Miss Greenfield left, Henry just stared at the girl in the mirror. "What father would want a son who looks like this?" she asked as she swished the tulle of her skirt.

She heard the door chime, some echoes of conversation, and then her mother's dreaded voice rang out. "Henry! Robert is here! Don't keep your young man waiting!"

After weeks of practice, Henry was fairly adept at walking in heels, but these were thinner and taller than anything that she had worn in the past month so she made sure to hold the bannister, as she made her way down the curving steps of the house. Pausing at her mother's insistence several times while she snapped pictures.

Robert was in a black tux with a green tie that matched Henry's dress. As Henry made her way down the stairs, Robert's smile looked like the toothy maw of a predator.

"Now over here, both of you!" Henry's mom motioned to the study with its roaring fire and oak bookshelves. There she snapped pictures as Henry pinned a flower on Robert's tux and Robert slid a corsage made of white and green flowers up Henry's wrist. "Hold each other's hands and look into each other's eyes! Good!" She snapped pictures and gave out instructions. "Now Henry, turn around, Robert, put your arm around her! Good! Now side by side, pull her close! GREAT!"

As Henry's mom looked at her phone to review her snapshots, Robert's hand slid off Henry's waist and squeezed her ass through her skirt. "Gotta thong under there sissy?" He asked in a low voice.

Henry glanced up but neither Miss Greenfield or his mother had seen. "None of your business" Henry grumbled.

"I'll know soon enough. It is prom night after-all.'" He gave Henry's ass one more squeeze before taking her by the hand and leading her out the door to a waiting black stretch Limo.

As they approached, the driver opened the door and Henry saw that Chad Melvin and his date Stacy Chambers were already there.

"Aww, Sissy Henry looks so pretty!" Chad called out as Henry climbed in.

"She definitely looks like Robert's type!" Stacy replied. The two of them laughed.

Robert slid in beside Henry and the door closed. Robert put his hand on Henry's thigh at the top of her stocking. "She looks good enough to eat!" he said as he leaned over and nibbled Henry's ear while his hand slid up Henry's thigh and brushed against Henry's cage.

Henry tried to slide away, but there was nowhere to go.

"Please!" Henry pleaded.

"So I should send that video from the bathroom to your mom and Miss Greenfield?" Robert asked.

Henry remembered what Miss Greenfield had just said. Whatever happened, he would be blamed for Robert's actions. "No!" Henry said hurriedly.

"Then be a good girl tonight and no one needs to know." Stacy lifted her phone and started recording as Robert took Henry by the chin, and kissed her, pushing his tongue into Henry's mouth, pinning her against the side of the car as they pulled away.

The Prom was held in the ballroom of a nearby hotel. Robert spent the entire 10 minutes of the drive pawing at Henry's caged cock and making out with her while Stacy recorded it all "For insurance". He unzipped his fly and guided Henry's hand to his dick, "Stroke it sissy!" he demanded.

As Henry rubbed Robert's dick, Chad leaned over to Stacy. "Why don't you give me a hand job too?"

"Hang on!" Stacy said. "Rob needs this footage, I'll blow you later."

"Yeah!" Rob grunted. "Sissy Henry's gonna be a good girl for her man if she doesn't want this getting out!"

Henry closed her eyes in shame as he felt Rob's dick get even harder in her hand.

When they arrived, Henry was using a napkin to wipe cum off her hand and then had to reapply her lipstick before they went inside.

All eyes were on Henry and phones were out and ready, in case she dared break femininity for a moment. She danced with Robert, gasping for what little air his corset would allow.

As the ballots went around, Henry was sitting on Robert's lap. Robert's hand went up Henry's skirt, and his finger was stroking the gaps in Henry's cock-cage. To Henry's shame she could feel the familiar ache of a constrained erection against the cage.

Chad held up his ballot and leaned in close. "We should write in Sissy Henry for Prom Queen!"

Robert laughed. "You think we could get the votes?"

"I'll hit the other tables, and see if we can at least get her on as a runner-up" Chad replied.

Stacy grabbed his hand. "Don't you dare!" She demanded. "I have a shot, but not if your friends all throw away their votes on that freak-show!"

Chad slumped.

"Well, she is getting one vote! That will at least get her in the school paper!" Robert announced. "Put Sissy Henry on the ballot!" He demanded. "Spelled just like that"

Henry looked at him for mercy, but he only continued to rub Henry's cock-cage. One-voters were the joke of the school every year. The pathetic losers who voted for themselves but had no friends. Now Henry would join their ranks. Resigned she wrote “Sissy Henry as instructed.

Chad grinned wide, swiped the slip from the table and rushed away.

A slow song began to play and Robert took Henry out to the middle of the floor. At the end of the song, Henry saw that a circle of spectators had formed around them and many had their phones out. Robert dipped Henry deep, allowing her skirt to fall in double slits exposing her thigh high stockings to the room and then pulled her up into a deep kiss before taking her ass in his hand to lead her back to the table where Henry had to return to her place on Robert’s lap with Robert’s hand back up her skirt.

After the ballots were counted, and Janet Speilmen crowned queen, Stacy had no desire to stay. There was an after-party already underway at the Cushing house and she convinced Chad and Robert it was time to go.

As soon as they were in the car, Chad and Stacy began to make out. Robert pushed Henry down onto their seat and climbed on top, making out with him and sliding his hand up and down Henry’s freshly shaved leg while dry humping her. Henry looked at the car ceiling and cried.

When they arrived, Henry was surprised to see Wendy dressed casually and smoking a cigarette outside the house.

“I didn’t see you at the dance.” Henry said.

“No date” Wendy replied and then her eyes dodged

over to Robert who had his hand on Henry's ass and was leading him inside.

"Help me" Henry mouthed to her, then Robert pulled her through the door.

Inside the house, the music was as loud as at the Prom. Lights were dim and Henry could smell pot and beer. Couples were making out on the couch, the recliners and even on the floor.

Chad and Stacy went straight up stairs.

"It's too loud here!" Robert yelled and led Henry through the house past everyone and onto the back patio where a cluster of athletes were gathered around the keg.

"Sissy Henry is in the house!" One of the jocks yelled as they emerged. "Looking good sissy!"

The whole group let out a series of whistles and hoots.

"Spin around for the boys!" Robert demanded as he lifted Henry's hand over her head.

Humiliated, Henry spun as commanded, letting her tulle skirt swish in the wind.

"DAMN! That Sissy's hotter than most of the real girls at this dump!" One of the guys cried out.

"Too bad she don't have a pussy!" Another cried.

"Boy pussy is in the rear!" A third announced. "How bout it Rob! Gonna give it to her boy-pussy?"

Henry looked at the guys terrified and then up at Rob who was smiling.

"Look how scared she is!" Robert laughed as he reached around and grabbed Henry's ass. She could feel the boy's finger pushing up between her cheeks. "She's so puckered up I can't even get my finger up there!"

"Relax Sissy!" Yelled one of the jocks. "Take it like a girl!"

"Spread those cheeks Henry!" Another mocked.

Henry was shaking her head. Sweat beading and running down the sides of her face. "No." she pleaded.

Robert stopped laughing. "Did you say no to me?"

"Please Robert!" Henry begged.

Robert pulled Henry close and gripped her by the arms. "Did the word 'NO' come out of your sissy little mouth?"

"No," Henry said again.

Robert looked around and then back at Henry. "They need to see what your sissy mouth is for! On your knees!"

Henry looked around. The yard had gone silent. Every eye was on them, staring at her in her green dress and corset being told to suck a boy's dick. She shook her head. This was too far. No one could expect her to do this. No one could make her!

"Suck it, or I'll send it!" He demanded and then started to try and push Henry down.

Something snapped.

Fear, anger, and desperation all took control of Henry as she lifted his knee straight into Robert's Crotch while yelling "NO!"

Robert fell to his knees in shock.

Henry reared her high-heeled foot back and swung again with all her might. The kick caught the boy's

crotch, lifted Robert off the ground and splayed him backwards as he let out a high pitched scream. The Jocks charged in and pinned Henry down.
Robert kept screaming holding his crotch "It burst! Oh GOD! HELP!"
Someone called 911
Wendy took out her phone and called her parents.

Henry had the holding cell to herself. Earlier in the morning, there had been a collection of drunks and scum. Some left her alone, others couldn't help but wonder why a pretty girl in a prom dress was in the men's cell until Henry spoke. Then they called her a sissy or worse and laughed. After the past month, it was just more of the same for Henry.
When the guards escorted Henry out, she saw her Mom and Miss Greenfield waiting for her. Behind them, her father was red-faced. He took one look at his son in the pretty dress, turned and left shaking his head.
"We know everything now," Henry's mom said.
"What do you mean?" Henry asked.
"Not a word, young lady!" Her mom said sternly.
Miss Greenfield nodded with approval.
The drive back to the house was silent. The bright morning light reminded Henry how tired she was, having not slept yet. When they arrived at the house, a black imported sedan was also in the driveway.
"Go get into your chores uniform then find us

in the study" Miss Greenfield demanded as they entered.

Henry didn't argue.

Dressed in the frilly French Maid Dress, Henry pushed open the sliding door to see her Father, Mother, Miss Greenfield, Wendy, her parents, and two other women, one in a lab coat, one in a suit were all sitting around the room. One of the leather wingback chairs was empty in the middle of the room.

"Henry, Sit down!" Her mother instructed.

Henry crossed to the chair and sat, crossing her legs in their patterned stockings nervously.

Henry's father took a deep breath and then sighed. "Wendy here, just told us the most astonishing story." He said. "About how she lied about your girlfriend's abortion. She said she was trying to avoid getting fixed up with you!"

Henry looked with relief over at Wendy. She had finally told the truth and this was all going to be over! Then he saw Wendy's puffy eycs, her look of despair.

"She said that you begged her to tell us this sooner!" Henry's Dad continued. "Is this true?"

Henry nodded. "Yes sir."

His dad took another breath, almost seething. "You asked?" He said again.

"YES!" Henry insisted.

His Dad's neck tightened, veins visible. "No real man would ask a woman to lie for him like that."

Henry's eyes went wide. "Dad! I didn't.." Henry

began

His Dad held his hand up to silence him. He turned to Wendy. “Young lady, your devotion to your friends is admirable, but nothing is gained by telling falsehoods. I’m sorry you felt that you needed to be involved.” He nodded to Wendy’s parents who took her by the hand and led her out of the room.

“Dad! Please!” Henry tried again.

“You expected me to believe that crap?” He spun on Henry. “You spoiled, pathetic, sissy!”

“THEY MADE ME!” Henry shouted back as he leapt to his feet.

The slap startled him and sent him back down into his chair.

“They made you berate Wendy in front of the whole school? They made you give Robert a hand-job? They made you put that poor boy in the hospital after you led him on?” His dad barked out the accusations.

“Hospital?” Henry asked as he rubbed his stinging cheek.

“Ruptured testicles” His mother said. “You castrated him.”

“He tried to force me!” Henry complained.

“We all saw the videos little-one” Miss Greenfield said. “The Limo ride, the dance floor, sitting at the table. You led him on.”

“You little slut!” Henry’s Dad said. “And when you changed your mind, you ruined him. Now his family wants to ruin us.”

"You will be convicted Henry. There are half a dozen videos of you assaulting him." His mother said. "Then there are the civil penalties. Robert is sterile now, the settlement will be in the millions! Your entire inheritance. When you get out of prison you will be broke, and don't expect help from us!"

"He forced me," Henry said meekly.

Henry's Dad threw his hands up in exasperation. "She's all yours!" He declared as he stormed out of the room.

"DAD!" Henry got up to follow.

"Sit down, young lady!" Miss Greenfield's stern voice demanded.

Henry shot a harsh look at her. This was all her fault. "Why should I listen to you?" She demanded. "This is all your fault! Now I have nothing to lose, so you can just fuck all the way off!"

"You still have choices young lady!" Henry's Mother said. "Sit down and listen because this is important!" She nodded to the woman in the suit who brought forward an envelope stuffed with papers and set them on a round table that she moved in front of Henry's chair.

Henry's mother continued. "Miss Landry here is one of our lawyers. She and Robert's family lawyer have worked hard to come to an agreement, one that you will need to sign."

Henry looked down at the envelope the top of one sheet was sticking out. It read;

"FORM FOR CHANGING SEX DESIGNATION"

"What is this?" Henry asked as he pulled the papers out.
"That is your future, little lady!" Henry's mother explained. "Your only future that has any hope."
Miss Greenfield picked up. "Robert and his family are pissed! They want you to pay for what you did to their son."
His Mother went on. "At the same time, Your father and I have decided that you are unfit to be a man."
Henry flipped through the pages. In addition to a settlement with Robert's family, it included Medical releases, and name change forms. The last page was a new College Enrollment form. His eyes fell to the name. "Hailey?"
"You are going to transition, Little-One" Miss Greenfield said. "Legally, Socially and Physically."
"No!" Henry pleaded.
"Say no, and there is no college, no money, and no future. Just a prison cell and a lifetime in debt." His mother explained.
"How?" Henry asked.
Miss Grenfield smiled. "You have already begun your social transition. We will continue through the summer as we had already planned, only now you will also be starting hormones. As soon as school gets out, you will have an orchiectomy, that means that your testicles will be surgically removed. Robert's family wanted it sooner but we convinced them to let you graduate intact. Once your testicles are gone, the hormones should kick into high gear and we should be seeing real

changes by the time you start college in the fall."

"You will be in the girl's dorm, of course," Henry's mom explained. "Wendy will be your roommate. She will take over for Miss Greenfield in teaching you how to be a girl"

Henry nodded. Wendy would be a welcome escape.

"We'll want to see what estrogen and progesterone do on their own," Miss Greenfield said. "So you will have a couple years between your orchi and any other surgeries, but the settlement with Robert's family includes a generous minimum cup size requirement and it's probably going to take surgical augmentation to get you there. They also insisted that you have bottom surgery before you get your degree." She shrugged. "Robert's Father's exact words were, If she gets to graduate highschool with her balls, she won't finish college with a dick!"

Henry felt her face tingle. She looked down at the papers. She tried to imagine what it would be like to be a girl, to lose her dick and have real giant tits. She was terrified. Then she remembered the holding cell last night, years in prison and the dreadful unknown that would follow. Wouldn't it be better to face a future with an education and an inheritance, no matter what was between her legs? She picked up the pen.

The woman in the lab coat came forward and opened a case on the desk across from Henry. It contained alcohol wipes, rows of vials marked

"Estradiol" and a stack of disposable syringes. She began to draw up Hailey's first dose.

Ghost in the Sex Machine

The hospital data structure appeared as a collection of glowing rectangles laid out on the electric blue plane of the cyberscape. Corwin watched from an adjacent public node as authorized users passed in and out of its gateways until he found his prey, Dr. Elwood Hastings, Chief of staff. His credentials would become his golden ticket!

Corwin executed a “Shoulder-tap daemon” as Elwood authenticated, then ran through multiple AI assisted decryption cycles before painting Corwin’s avatar with a perfect replica. Confident, he presented himself to the Cyber-gate and passed inside. Too easy!

In his one room apartment across from the Hospital, Corwin lay in a folding lawn chair, eyes closed, arms at his side, hard linked via a cluster of nanofiber cables from the I/O port behind his ear to his data-terminal that lay across his lap. He grinned.

Corwin was a mesh-jumper. A computer expert who used the hyper-reactive brain-machine interface of his cybernetic neuromesh to connect his mind directly to the web, removing the impediments of keyboards, mice and touchscreens and allowing him to work at the speed of thought. He was also an extortionist, his specialty was the capture and ransom of vital data. His trade moved no product, crossed all borders, and could be extremely profitable if the buyer was motivated. He would secure the mark’s data, lock it behind encryption, then sell the key for a set price in crypto currency deposited in a single-use data-vault. It had been so lucrative that he had dropped out of school ten years ago and been on his own since.

But Corwin knew that his luck couldn't last forever, he needed one big score he could live on and "retire" at 24. That meant he needed a target with the deepest pockets and the greatest motivation.

Government and banking data structures were suicide, they spent almost as much on data security as on executive compensation. Corwin had to think outside the box.

Midas Hospital Systems was the largest for-profit healthcare provider in the world, and this location treated some of the most elite of the 1%. The patient data vault, containing their treatment plans, would be something MHS would pay almost anything to retain, and Hospital Data Security was not something anyone in the mesh-jumping community ever talked about.

Corwin had spent the last week exploring the hospital in meat-space while pretending to be a new patient in the cash-clinic, and then returning daily to "discuss" his bill. Irritated desk clerks had sent him bouncing from department to department, which excused his wandering the halls while he scanned the physical structure of the on-prem internal cloud the Hospital maintained..

Now, knowing the physical layout of the building, the organizational layout of the staff and the digital layout of the cyber-compound, Corwin had set up within broadcast range to initiate his run.

Digitally disguised as Dr. Hastings in cyberspace, Corwin passed through the administrative layers of hospital daily operation and made his way directly to his prize, A glowing red cube in the middle of the virtual compound, the "PHI Vault." His avatar was admitted through the first layer but inside the first layer he hit a biometric second-factor interrogation protocol.

In his apartment, Corwing swiped his finger across the pad, the dermal-patch made from samples he had taken from Hastings in person a day ago should do their trick.

"FAILED"

He swiped again.

"FAILED"

Cautious of triggering any alerts, Corwin did not try a third time, He disengaged from the PHI Vault, cycled away one grid unit and observed.

AI constructs, representing complex claims and treatment systems, moved fluidly through the barricade unhindered. Corwin would have to go to plan B.

Digital Engram Clone Constructs (DECCs) were virtual copies of people, disconnected from their physical bodies. From a DECC's perspective, they were real people, with memories and feelings. DECC Personhood was not legally recognized and cyberspace was full of despondent disembodied DECCs squatting in abandoned data-storage, forgotten or even rejected by the physical originals who had created them, in some cases the original person was dead and the DECC was a literal "ghost" in the machine space. Corwin hated the idea of spawning a DECC and every time he did so he was careful to take steps toward preserving what he considered "continuity of consciousness."

Corwin would instruct his console to put him under, for the DECC run. His construct would go in, trigger his encryption bomb, then return with the key-data to his mesh-link and upload the record of its experiences and reintegrate before Corwin awoke. From his perspective, he would have done it all personally and no DECC would be left behind. He set his DECC up for an 8hr auto-dissolve to correspond with the sleep protocol he was triggering through his console. If his DECC had not uploaded back to a physical construct by that time, it would simply fade away.

Confident that he was ready, he punched in the execution command and then felt his consciousness slip away.

Again, Corwin was looking out at the Hospital's virtual compound. The typical double-body sensation he usually felt on a run was missing, he had no hands to type with or face to grin with. He was an entirely virtual being and he understood that he was the DECC.

No time to get existential, if did this right, he

could, from his own frame of reference, return to his body as soon as this job was done.

Almost before he thought of it, a virtual assistance tag was manufactured by his intrusion software and layered over his Dr. Elwood Hastings authentication mask. Now he looked like Dr. Hasting's AI assistant, part of the machine, authorized to act as the Doctor with no physical body thus no biometric check.

He passed through the external gateway once more, moving faster than a physical mind could have processed, it was almost a teleport! His reactions and sensations were all digital now, and he was operating far beyond the capabilities of a meat-brain. The PHI barrier swelled before him and he felt the gentle warmth of its security scan as he passed through without effort.

He was there! Rows and rows of patient data, treatment plans, medical histories, and drug interactions all arrayed into easy access tables around him. He queried the name of an eccentric billionaire, instantly every detail of his physical health and that of his family hovered in space before him. Access beyond Corwin's wildest dreams. He considered pulling copies, but that's not what he was here for.

The Encryption bomb was non-destructive to the data around him. Triggered, it would swell over the access layer that surrounded this vault and harden into an impenetrable shell unless released by the encryption key Corwin would sell them. In

Cyberspace, he imagined it as a glowing orb that he now manifested in front of him.

Everything turned red!

Before Corwin could trigger the orb it was encased in what looked like a reflective darkness. Corwin recoiled in horror immediately! Lethal intrusion countermeasures. "Black ice" The artificially intelligent defense would immediately snap-shot then destroy any unauthorized code it encountered. Corwin was currently nothing but unauthorized code. His "true self" was safe asleep in the apartment, if he was deleted as a DECC, that would not change, but, Corwin the DECC would experience it as a death,and he did not know if a DECC could experience pain, what was worse was that the snapshot would lead authorities right up his data stream. Cops would kick down his door before his sleep protocol was resolved.

He needed to get out and back to his body now!

As fast as he could move in DECC form, he could sense the Black Ice moving faster around him. He projected himself toward the gateway but before he got there, he saw the black shimmering representation of its power solidify around the portal. He was locked inside the Hospital net and it was only a matter of time before the Black Ice closed around him!

He needed shelter fast and a way to physically leave the network! Maybe cybernetics, something he could move in the physical world? The department portals were already closed off! He retreated from the black Ice that surrounded him. Back into Elwood Hasting's department, back into his personal network, into his office.

The solution was waiting for him in a glowing node that denoted a fully autonomous AI operated cybernetic frame.

It was labeled "ExecAdmin-Rachel" and it had the open active memory space for his entire DECC image.

As the Black Ice closed around him, he dove out of cyberspace and into the "Rachel" node.

Corwin blinked. He had been past this room before but not seen it from this perspective. Something obscured part of his vision. A slender feminine hand with ruby red nails rose up and brushed a strand of hair out of the way and behind a delicate ear. He looked down and saw a white silk blouse stretched near bursting over large perky breasts. Looking around again, Corwin realized he was seated at the reception desk outside Dr. Hasting's office in the body of the sexy assistant he had ogled several times as he had been casing the hospital. Dr. Elwood Hastings' executive admin was an AI operated bio-droid. Artificial flesh and blood operated by a digital brain and now Corwin was in the co-pilot's seat.

Corwin shifted weight and felt an odd sensation down below Rachel's legs rubbed together, smooth and hairless and nothing was between them. It was disorienting for an instant as Corwin opened and closed Rachel's legs again, closing completely without the impediment of a penis and testicles that Corwin was used to. If he opened Rachel's legs wide enough he could feel...open.

There was no time to explore! Corwin was no longer a DECC and vulnerable to Black Ice deletion, but if he did not make physical I/O link between this bio-droid and his console before his body awoke from it's cyber-induced sleep, continuity of consciousness would be broken and he would never be able to reintegrate. Corwin the human would have no memory of this run, and be unaware of his danger as the police closed in. Worse, Corwin the DECC's auto delete protocol only applied in the net-run. Now that he had transferred into this Rachel-bot his image was perpetual. From his perspective, he would remain a disembodied ghost doomed to wander the net for eternity with all the other abandoned DECC's now sheltered in the cloud. Or worse, he could be stuck in the body of this bimbo-bot. Quickly, Corwin detached the IO Cable from the deck on Rachel's desk and stood. He took a step toward the door, turned an ankle on 3" heels and toppled to the floor!

MINOR DAMAGE DETECTED
LEFT ANKLE
MOBILITY COMPROMISED
ISOLATING CONFLICTING MOTOR IMPULSE

The text quickly scrolled through Corwin's field

of view. He tried to move his arm but nothing happened. "SHIT! Stand up" he thought.

Suddenly, arms pushed Corwin up from the ground into a crouch, then stood, smoothing the miniskirt down at the same time. Rachel was obeying Corwin's instructions but she had cut off his direct control of her body. He could still feel everything, but was operating her at a command line level rather than through direct interface.

"Raise hand" Corwin tested.

Rachel gently lifted her hand, palm open and out in front of her. Not what Corwin had intended, she was following her internally programmed motor instructions. He needed to get her out of here now!

"Go into the hallway" he commanded, then let Rachel begin to take short graceful strides, heel-toe, hips swaying, breast bouncing across the floor toward the door.

"Rachel! Where are you going?" Dr. Elwood Hasting's voice called from his office behind her.

"Ignore that" Corwin commanded.

Rachel ignored him. "To the hallway sir!" She answered.

"No sweetie," Hastings replied. "I could use some relaxation. Come in here and lock the door"

"No! No! No!" Corwin commanded!

Rachel turned and smiled at Elwood. He was a rather fit man with salt and pepper hair that matched his neatly trimmed beard. His shoulders were broad and he clearly spent time in the gym. He returned a lopsided grin as his blue eyes swept up and down her body. He raised one large muscular hand off his desk and motioned her over. Corwin could feel her getting wet as lubrication protocols were triggered and she licked her lips. As the body was flooded with waves of arousal, Corwin realized that Rachel was clearly far more than a simple bimbo-bot. Dr. Hastings had vat-grown her body to be almost human, then apparently enhanced it with sensory and performance enhancers. It was as though she was designed to host digital constructs. Rachel would feel and respond like a real woman but she would perform acts of pleasure beyond anything a mortal woman was capable of. Corwin was about to be the unwitting passenger of the world's most advanced sex-toy.

Rachel added more sway to her walk as she passed into his inner office, twirled so her pleated miniskirt flew up to expose that she wore no underwear, then pushed the door shut, turning the bolt.

As she did so, Elwood clicked a button on his computer initiating white noise generators in the outer office while low jazz music began to play around them.

Corwin didn't have time for this.

Corwin didn't have the stomach for this.

Corwin had always been a straight man.

He could recognize that the Doctor was a rather fit and good looking man, but that was purely objective judgment, he personally felt no attraction to him, or any other man. He had ever had an experimental phase, and now he was in the front seat of a pleasure drone about to go to work! Desperately he explored Rachel's internal systems for another network connection, a way he could go DECC Once more and get out of there!

"Abort Abort Abort" he kept commanding.

PRIORITY IS GIVEN TO ADMINISTRATOR
SECONDARY SYSTEM COMMANDS IGNORED

The text appeared to float in the air as Rachel made her way around the desk while unbuttoning her blouse.

Elwood turned his chair sideways and slid down so he was seated at the edge as Rachel knelt in front of him, her top was now open and she unclasped the hook in the middle of her bra. Everything Rachel wore was for the benefit of her master. Her bra seemed to burst open under the pressure of her massive tits, the fabric springing aside as Corwin felt their weight shift.

Elwood reached down and cupped them in his hands, massaging the nipples with his thumbs as he kneaded her flesh.

The sensitivity was something Corwin was not prepared for. Waves of pleasure washed over Rachel's body at Elwood's touch and Corwin experienced it all. He could hardly focus on the hardware inventory he was trying to run as he looked for any I/O Port to get him out of her before things got too serious!

Nothing! No Wi-Fi, no heartbeat to a central server,

not even a Universal Time Clock link. Without her skull-jack connected, Rachel was a completely isolated system. A system that was locking eyes with Elwood as she licked her lips and unhooked his belt.

Elwood lifted his but for a moment as Rachel pulled his pants and boxers down. His cock was now exposed in front of her, semi stiff. Corwin could smell him as Rachel leaned in closer.

"Oh God!" Corwin said to himself as he felt Rachel open her mouth and extend her tongue. She gently licked the tip of his penis, it was salty and rough. She brought her right hand up under his balls and cupped his scrotum. With her left hand she wrapped her slender fingers around his cock and began to stroke it slowly as she kissed the tip.

Corwin was horrified even as he felt the heat and tingle of Rachel's arousal, her body programmed to take pleasure in giving pleasure. As she parted her lips and wrapped them around his head, licking the underside of the tip while she stroked his shaft with her hand, Corwin felt him stiffen. At the same time, the tingle and heat in Rachel's crotch began to grow in surges. Corwin realized that Rachel had been customized with a Simul-Max reactive system, a simultaneous climax protocol that would give a pleasure drone an orgasm every time the owner had one. The more she stimulated Dr. Hastings, the more pleasure her body would feel.

The taste of the first drop of precum was

an unpleasant surprise for Corwin. Even when masturbating, he had never tasted semen before this moment. The bitter and salty flavor, the thick texture and the understanding of what it was would have made him gag if he had control of a throat at that moment.

Rachel, however, did exactly the opposite of what Corwin wanted her to do as she moved her hand off his cock to make way as she slid her mouth down on him. Corwin could feel him penetrate to the back of her mouth, she raised her shoulders to adjust her angle allowing his cock to push down her throat until her lips met the tuft of curly hair at the base.

Corwin could feel him thrust deeper, the throat relax in response, and her nose pressed into his belly.

Dr. Hasting's hands gripped either side of her head, palms on her ears. Corwin could feel her earrings pressing into her neck, He pulled her head up, then slammed it back down, again and again as he roughly fucked her face.

Rachel did nothing to protest. She was programmed to be used by him any way he wished. She put her hands on the base of his chair to steady herself as he bounced her on his cock.

"Let me hear you!" he commanded.

Corwin could feel her throat close slightly as she began to hum, the thrusting of his cock turning her humming into a repeated "Gluck, gluck, gluck" sound.

"Yeah! Take it!" he grunted.

His cock was hitting her throat hard, Corwin could feel that her jaw was starting to ache.

Suddenly he tightened his grip on her head, and threw her back so hard that she toppled backwards and landed on her back on the floor of his office.

Dr. Hastings grinned as he stood over her, his wet cock dripping precum and Rachel's synthetic saliva in a long string toward the floor. He toed his leather shoes off each foot and stepped out of the pants that had pooled around his ankles.

Rachel responded by laying back, bringing up her knees and opening her legs.

"Not yet my pet" Elwood's voice rumbled as he bent down and began to draw his thick leather belt out through the loops in his discarded pants. "Over the desk."

Rachel sat up and moved into a kneeling position, bending down and kissing the top of Dr. Hasting's feet. Corwin smelled the pungent odor and tasted the bitter skin, it was almost worse than a mouthful of cock.

She rose, slowly, ceremonially, turned toward the desk, pressed her pelvis to it and bent down so that her breasts were pressed down on the mahogany surface. She brought her arms forward in front of her and gripped the far edge of the desk, moving her feet apart.

Corwin could feel her skirt being lifted, exposing her bare ass. The rough skin of Dr. Elwood's palm caressed her ass and probed down between her legs. Corwin's mind spun at the alien sensation of a man's fingers pressing in between Rachel's labia. Corwin could feel Elwood stroke the threshold, feel the wetness, the sliding of his lubricated digits, the sparks of pleasure as he brushed her clit. Rachel gasped and Corwin quailed inside her mind as the fingers thrust inside her. Corwin could feel them curl and probe deeper, brushing the cervix, striking a spot that caused pleasure to echo and radiate out from her pelvis, up into her belly and down her legs. Heat and sparks and energy Corwin had never felt before.

Both Rachel and Corwin sighed in ecstasy at once and then his fingers pulled away, out of her, as Elwood stepped back.

In anticipation, Rachel gripped the edge of the desk tight. There was a whistle in the air and then a sharp blast of intense pain across her ass! Corwin reeled in confusion, the air whined again and another line of pain ripped up from a new welt as Rachel's ass rocked forward. Dr Hastings was whipping her with his belt!

<Whoosh> SNAP!

Rachel bit her lip, but Corwin felt the corners of her mouth twist up into a smile. She was enjoying this agony!

<Whoosh> SNAP!

She let out a high pitched squeak. Corwin desperately tried to seize control.

<Whoosh> SNAP!

The one was across her back, she caught her

breath for a moment. Corwin tried to find a way to edit the sensory feed from his connection, but he wasn't protected by any layers of hardware, as a DECC he was pure interface and completely unfiltered.

<Whoosh> SNAP!

The top of her thighs this time! Why was she just taking this? Corwin could feel her growing more wet as the blows fell. The damned thing was programmed to be a pain-slut!

<Whoosh> SNAP!

STOP IT! STOP IT! STOP IT!

Corwin was under a sensory overload, the pain from the welts, the heat and numbness between them, the arousal of the body, the taste of cum and sweat in her mouth. He was unable to process it all and helpless to filter it.

<Whoosh> SNAP!

The arousal! The wetness, the tingling of electricity, it all felt so good. Corwin focused on the pleasure still radiating from Rachel's crotch through her body, suddenly aware of how it seemed to stretch tendrils of sensation everywhere. The pressure of her breasts on the desk, the shiver of her thighs. It was all so much more than Corwin had ever experienced sexually as a man and she hadn't even done the act yet!

<Whoosh> SNAP!

More red hot pain! More numbness in the shrinking space between welts, more heat and sparks along the line of impact, more tension in her crotch, more flexing of her legs. She was ready for it, wanted it, she never wanted the whipping to end.

The belt came down past Rachel's vision and closed into a collar around her neck. Elwood pulled, closing her airway and dragging her back up into a standing position. Rough hands spun her around to face him and he seemed ready to devour her.

He dropped the end of the belt, gripping either side of her blouse he pulled it down and off her shoulders while pushing her back. Rachel's butt was on the edge of the desk, she sat and used her hands to brace herself as he pushed her down onto her back. He pushed a knee between her legs and she opened for him, raising her legs on either side of the man and wrapping them around his waist.

His cock was hard and pointed to the ceiling. Rachel reached down with her right hand and gently pushed it down till the head aligned with her waiting cunt.

Dr. Hastings was gentle and slow as he pushed into her the first time. Rachel sighed gratefully while Corwin panicked inside her head. He could feel the cock sliding inside, the sense of fullness in a gap he never knew was there. The shiver and tingle of sensation as Dr. Hastings thrust deep inside, then back, then in once more, the rhythmic waves of growing pleasure with each stroke of his thrusting pump.

Corwin was in the body of a woman, being fucked

by a man who had just face-fucked and whipped her, to his own surprise, he was enjoying himself so much that he had forgotten to even check the clock on this run!

A quick look showed that it had been only 30 minutes since he had fled the ice into this body, but right now, laying on this desk, breasts bouncing with each thrust and Dr. Hasting's cock inside, time didn't matter!

Corwin gripped the side of the desk, and moaned. She shifted her hips to help the next thrust go deeper and was rewarded by new waves of greater pleasure.

Dr. Hastings grinned wide. "All mine" he said. "You want it?"

"Please!" Corwin moaned.

The waves built behind a damn Corwin could sense bulging inside her. A surging swell of sensation that grew greater with every thrust of Elwood's hips. She clenched her fists and felt her nails dig into her palms. A disembodied mind realized that direct control had returned.

Corwin didn't have to be here, on her back! Corwin could stop this, get up, run back to the apartment and end this DECC run. Corwin could finish the job. Corwin didn't care!

The surge of sensation was all that mattered in the moment. After the dam burst and the promised waves of pleasure washed over Rachel's body, after Corwin had fulfilled this moment, the rest of the mission could be completed, but for now, Corwin needed to be Rachel, she needed the cock inside her and she needed the climax that it promised.

She felt Elwood drive even deeper, gripping her thighs. She felt him pulse and the spurt of warm cum inside her and she felt the damn burst. A waterfall of ecstasy and pleasure as the cybernetically enhanced body shivered and quaked in magnified synchronous orgasm with her master.

"Ohhhhh GOD!" Corwin cried out through Rachel's red lips.

Elwood arched his back as he thrust deeper and moaned gratefully.

Corwin could feel him still pulsing inside her as the blast of pleasure drove away all reason and comprehension. Every part of the body was there, singing together in harmony a song that seemed to wash out from the surface between Elwood's cock and her pussy. Her lips quivered, her arms curled and she shook all over.

At last, Dr. Hastings sighed, and stepped backwards, pulling out of her. Corwin could feel his warm cum trail out of her and down her still burning ass cheeks. She just lay back and stared at the ceiling in disbelief at what she had just experienced.

"Well, now you're fucked" Dr. Hastings said as he unwrapped the belt from her neck.

"Yeah...." Corwin replied, the echoing sensations of orgasm still washing back and forth across her body.

Elwood smiled at her dazed response then looked down at his dripping cock. “Be a darling and lick that off for me please” he said.

Corwin winced at the idea and realized her shoulders tensed at the same time. He was back in control! He didn’t know how or why it happened, but at some point during intercourse, Corwin’s engram regained primary motor control!

Sitting up, Corwin could see Elwood leering with a wide smile while he took a long pull from a water bottle, his cock already growing erect once more. It was a given that Dr. Elwood Hastings would have the Zero-Refractory™ implants he helped develop. Combined with amped up prostate enhancements, the man could, in theory, shoot load after load to the point of dehydration and the way he was chugging water, that would not be happening any time soon. Corwin needed to get out of there now.

He jumped down off the desk, feeling a new stream of cum run down Rachel’s leg. He would grab Hastings by the balls, pull and twist to get him down, knock him out and make a run for it!

He swung forward, and felt the fingers of Rachel’s right hand gently wrap around Elwood’s dripping, stiff cock as Rachel licked her lips and lowered herself to her knees in front of her master.

Motor control was gone once more! Corwin was once again only a passenger as Rachel wrapped her lips around Dr. Hastings cock and began licking it clean. The faint hint of strawberries was mixed in with the salty bitterness of semen. It took Corwin by surprise for a moment till he figured it out. Rachel was a high end pleasure drone, top of the line with every apparent enhancement. Even the juices of her pussy were specially flavored for the pleasure of her master.

As she sucked and licked at his cock, Corwin felt her own body growing more aroused once more as the mirror-climax protocol triggered. Her nipples were hard as waves began to surge from her crotch where the tsunami had swept through just minutes ago. She reached up and cupped the man's testicles with her hand, gently stroking his sack.

Corwin accessed her internal chronometer, It had only been half an hour since the run had begun. Thirty minutes ago, Corwin had been a hot shot mesh-jumper about to make the score of a lifetime, now he was some female pleasure drone, getting wet as she robotically sucked a man's cock! How could so much have happened so quickly?

The waves grew faster in her as Hastings grabbed the top of her head and began pushing her farther down his cock, then back up, directing her as she undulated her tongue under his penis and varied the pressure she applied with her lips.

New drops of precum added to the flavor in her mouth and the swells of pleasure within her grew into giant surges.

She felt his cock twitch in her lips, his balls seemed to rise and then her mouth was awash in his cum. Pulse after pulse projected against the back of her throat and she swallowed without hesitation, gulping it down as the surges broke through into another wave of indescribable pleasure that washed over her once more.

The taste was awful but the sensation all consuming, Corwin swallowed the vile fluid and then collected the last trickles on her tongue. She slurped off the tip and sat back on her heels looking up at the man she had just blown swallowing once more. He was looking off into space, an expression Corwin knew well, Dr. Hastings was receiving a message on his optical implant, The image would be overlaid on his normal vision in real time augmented reality.

She still had the taste of his cum in her mouth. She swallowed a couple more times and tried to scrape her tongue against her upper teeth as she made a sour face.

Dr. Hastings came back into full awareness as she did this and touched her cheek. "It's a taste you need to get used to, Mr. Corwin Daws." Dr. Hastings cupped his hand under her chin tilting it up to look into her eyes. His grin broadened as Corwin's shocked expression expanded across Rachel's delicate features.

Corwin was back in control once more but what Dr. Hastings had just said left him frozen in shock and terror. How did Hastings know he was in Rachel? How did he know Corwin's name? What was the message he had just received?

"Who?" Corwin replied with Rachel's soft voice. "..Master" he added after a pause while wondering what speech protocols the drone ran under.

Dr. Hastings shook his head as he let go of her chin and stepped back. "Do you think you are the first person to try and steal from me, Mr. Daws?" He scooped his pants off the floor and folded them.

"I don't know what..." Corwin tried to plead.

"Oh stop it!" Dr. Hastings demanded. "You are the digital construct of the criminal jumper Corwin Daws. You ran afoul of our ICE and were corralled into my Rachel unit to get off the network. Your datastream interfaced with her..." He looked into the middle distance as he checked his optical data once more "forty two minutes ago! Since then, you have been trying to figure out how to drive that body out of my hospital, across the street to the third floor apartment where your unconscious body lay so you could reintegrate consciousness before you woke up causing a dual-stream. I assume you find the obvious paradox of two sets of memories across the same time period disorienting."

In all of Corwin's life, he had been lucky to never have a close call, never be held accountable, never get caught. This was a new experience layered on a dozen other new experiences as he knelt in a woman's body, cum on her lips and running down her leg, at the mercy of a man who knew exactly who he was and what he had done.

He felt burning, moisture and pressure in Rachel's eyes and realized he was starting to cry.

Dr. Hastings tilted his head unsympathetically.

"Tears? I forgot I gave her those."

"How?" Corwin managed to say. Rachel's airway was choked shut, she felt like there was a lump of burning coal in the back of her throat. "How did you...."

"You are not nearly as clever as you think you are Mr. Daws." Dr. Hastings said as he moved to the wet bar across the office from where Corwin knelt.

Corwin seized the opportunity and made Rachel's body spring to her feet. She took two steps toward the door before Dr. Hastings shouted "Nadu!"

Motor control was yanked away, and helplessly Corwin felt the body turn and lower herself back down. She opened her legs, knees far apart and placed her hands on her thighs, palms up. She bowed her head and looked at a spot of carpet between her knees.

"Not clever at all," Dr. Hastings sighed. "The body you inhabit is my property and I have full command override. Rachel might let you drive from time to time, but only so long as you don't do anything to violate her programming."

Corwin screamed, nothing happened. Rachel held her submissive pose as Dr. Hastings circled her, sipping a whiskey and continuing his monologue.

"You didn't look too closely at my profile when you pulled my access. Had you done so, you would have found the big black redacted parts of my military record. While other doctors spent the DisWar patching men up, I spent it burrowing into their minds, finding out all the secret things that make us unique! A lot of what we have today is a result of my work. The neuromesh you use, the DECC you rode here, and the uplink channels that brought you into Rachel. I paved the way to where you are now. I also learned a thing or two about security." He swallowed the rest of his drink and set it down on his desk. "Let him speak Rachel"

Corwin moved her jaw and felt it respond. "Please let me go? I'll just reintegrate and then you can arrest me!"

Dr. Hastings picked up the glass once more and twirled it, watching the ice circle the bottom. "I'm afraid it's too late for that Mr. Daws. You see, the black ICE you encountered was a hunter-killer."

"Oh God" Corwin mumbled.

"You are familiar." Dr. Hastings shrugged. "It ran back up the data stream you entered through and found your deck. My security team arrived a few minutes later. They just confirmed that your synapses are fried. There is nothing but a mindless vegetable in that apartment. I can show you the image feed if you like."

"NO!" Corwin's cry in Rachel's high pitched breathy voice failed to match the despair he felt. He was dead, and the part of him, trapped inside this artificial woman, was only a ghost! Corwin wanted to wail, to thrash, to strike out at the man that killed him, but Rachel's body was still frozen in its submissive pose. "YOU BASTARD!" he cried.

""Corwin Daws is dead. You're only software, installed on my hardware. You belong to me!"

"Fuck you!" Corwin spat the words out, but they hardly sounded threatening in Rachel's seductive tones.

"Orgasm," Dr. Hastings said.

Without warning, waves of explosive pleasure suddenly crashed over Corwin. Rachel's body slumped and then fell backwards, bringing her knees up as her hands cupped her sex while she writhed in absolute ecstasy. "Un Nghhhh Ahhh" Corwin strained to focus and failed.

At last the waves receded leaving her twitching on the carpet, her hands soaked with her own fluids.

"Again!" Dr. Hastings commanded.

Before Corwin could take a deep breath he was moaning once more as another explosion of sensation rocked Rachel's form. Again, she writhed on the carpet until it receded.

Crowin rolled over onto her belly and tried to get up, rising to her hands and knees, panting in the aftermath.

"Again!"

Dr. Hastings said as he smacked her ass.

Corwin's arms buckled and she was face down on the floor as her hips gave way under the new orgasmic surge that flowed through her. She banged on the carpet in delight. Or was it frustration? Corwin couldn't remember if he wanted it to stop or if this was the best night of his life. As the wave crested and rolled back, Corwin rolled over onto her back, legs open and let out a satisfied sigh.

"Do you want another?" Dr. Hastings asked.

Corwin bit her lip and nodded.

Dr. Hastings, smiled and looked down at his cock, wet with her saliva and still pointing at the ceiling. Corwin followed his gaze and knew what it meant. All of his fear and anger seemed far away as her legs opened more and her knees rose up to welcome him. Corwin cursed the Rachel-body protocols that had agreed to this, and then admitted to himself that he had been in complete physical control of the body since the orgasms started. Sr. Hastings was the man that had killed him. Corwin should by trying to disable his voice so he can't activate Rachel. He should aim a punch at Dr. Hasting's neck! He would need the Dr. closer for that to work. Yes, that was the only reason she was laying back for him.

The Doctor knelt between her legs and stroked her thighs. He bent down and kissed her knee.

Corwin sighed in contentedness at his touch and the gentle brush of his lips.

He placed his hands on the carpet on either side of her and began to lower himself.

Just a little closer.

She looked at Adam's apple, right there. Her eyes drifted up and locked with his. She could feel the mirrored arousal surging with her. She licked her lips.

He bent down and kissed her as he entered her.

She did not strike. She was a woman enjoying the sensation of her lover inside her, thrusting and surging. She moved her hips, trying to draw him in deeper, faster, harder. Sex as a man was a pale shadow of this. This was so much better and she wanted it! She wanted him! She wanted the orgasm that was surging within her to break. She wanted to feel his hot cum inside. The gush and the trickle! She forgot that she was a man for that moment and thought of herself only as a sexual entity. Her desperation for sensation washed away her anger and despair. This is what she was now!

It struck, greater than before, amplified by the orgasms that had come before, as she felt him pulse and spurt her own body shuddered uncontrollably. Her arms flopped against the floor, her feet shivered as they hovered in the air and she screamed.

He was panting too. He stopped thrusting but remained inside her, and remained hard. "That was you." he whispered. "You chose that, didn't you?"

Still reeling as surges of sensation receded and her fingers tingled as though they had been asleep, she looked up at the man on top of her and shamefully nodded. Corwin had been in complete control of the body that had so welcomed him into her. The body that, even now, rolled her hips, wanting him to start pumping once more. Corwin wanted to be fucked again, wanted to be fucked forever. She never wanted this to end.

"I should hate you," She whispered. She was confused, lost, being a woman under him, around him, felt so right.

He stroked her forehead and kissed it. "But you don't, do you?"

"Yes I do." She undercut her own statement by shifting her hips, pushing him deeper into her. She knew she was lying. "You altered my code."

He raised himself up and drove his pelvis forward into her. She felt impaled on him and gasped in satisfaction. "I would never alter a single bit of your engram my dear. A mesh jumper like you is far too valuable intact!"

"Then why?" Corwin paused, ashamed to admit it. "Why do I want this? I'm a man!"

Dr. Hastings pulled back and thrust again as he stroked her breast. He bent down, took her nipple between his lips and stroked it with his tongue, then sucked her. To her surprise she felt fluid flow out of her into his mouth. The Rachel body had been modified to lactate, her milk was probably flavored just like her cunt. He picked up his head and swallowed. "Do you feel like a man any more?" He thrust his cock into her a few more times to make his point.

Her mouth hung open and she let out a squawk and shuddered. "No." she admitted.

He stroked her cheek. "The man is dead. You are my woman now."

Corwin felt tears roll down her cheek. "You killed me!"

"Our countermeasures are automated. You chose to step into their path." His dick twitched inside her.

"I'm nothing! Just a data ghost" She looked at him for sympathy.

His smile was warm. "You are Rachel, my assistant, and my lover"

"Your sexbot!" She said bitterly.

"Yes, if you choose to be." He said as he bent forward and nibbled her earlobe.

"Choice?" She asked.

"Corwin Daws is braindead, but his cybernetic mesh maintains his autonomic functions. The body still lives." Dr. Hastingswhispered. "I could install a system core linked to that mesh like the one in Rachel and implant your engram."

"I could live again?" Corwin's voice carried hope.

"You would be driving your own corpse around. Corwin Daws would be as dead as he is now." Dr, Hastings specified. "You would be a meat puppet, drifting through the same meaningless existence you had before, but I'll hold the strings. Whatever you choose, you belong to me." He held her gaze sternly to make sure she understood.

Corwin thought of waking up tomorrow in his own body, knowing he would be the digital undead. Still poor, still lonely and forever under the thumb of a man who could shut him off with a single command.

"Or," Dr. Hastings said as he began to slowly pump his hips, sending renewed waves of pleasure up from her cunt and through her body. "You accept your role as Rachel. Valued, pampered, pleasured,

beautiful and immortal. You will still jump for me. I need someone of your skills at my disposal either way." His thrusting grew faster, more rhythmic. She began to pant in time with his body.
"Be Rachel, or be Corwin!" He grunted, "Make your choice now!" His thrusting had grown frenzied, his face was a mask of intensity.
She felt him release again, and at the same moment the building climax washed over her she screamed out her answer.

Every year, the hospital held a "friendly ghost" halloween festival in the children's ward while the executives entertained the parents and VIPs at a costume ball upstairs.
Dr. Elwood Hastings stood at the entrance, his black hair slick back on his scalp with streaks of gray along the sides. He wore a 19th century nobleman's finery all in black with a long black cape, The artificial fangs grafted to his teeth and pale makeup completed his costume as the vampire king as he greeted the arriving guests.
He glanced at his companion and his broad smile looked more predatory than usual with the addition of his fangs. "Like clockwork," he said.
An older gentleman in a white suit, with a wig of bushy white hair and an artificial white mustache walked in and shook Elwood's hand.
"Major Hasting! It is so good to see you again!" The man beamed. "Dracula is a fitting look for you!"
"It's Doctor Hastings now, Mr. Secretary." Elwood

corrected. "Those days are long behind me." He looked the Secretary of Health up and down. "Samuel Clements I assume?"

The man beamed. "Mark Twain remains one of my favorites!" He shifted his attention. "But you have not introduced your lovely vampire queen!"

Rachel blushed and curtseyed, a movement her body had been programmed to do gracefully. She wore a black corset with black roses along the bust line and bottom fringe. She wore a ruffled crushed velvet miniskirt with a see through mesh skirt over it that came down to her ankles revealing her fishnet wrapped legs and spiked heeled boots. Over her slender shoulders, she had a satin and lace shawl that trailed a mesh cape behind her with small skulls printed in it. Her hair was black tonight and bundled up into a tight bun, giving her a severe look. She wore pale makeup made even more shocking by her blood red lipstick. Like Elwood, she wore artificial fangs, though hers could easily be removed for when she had to provide oral service to her master.

"This is Rachel, Mr. Secretary. She is an autonomous companion. Rachel, say hello to Health Secretary Ellison."

Secretary Ellison looked her up and down as he took her hand and kissed it.

"Hello Secretary Ellison" Rachel said seductively. Her bioscanner readout showed heightened excitement from the secretary as his hand lingered on hers. Tonight she would seduce him. Elwood would “lend” her to him as a gift. He would take her home, they would have their fun, and once the old man was satisfied and asleep, Rachel would link into his local network pulling down all the data Dr. Hastings desired.

She bit her lip as she imagined the pleasures her master would bestow on her when she returned. Corwin Daws was dead. She was Rachel now, and her unlife was better than anything Corwin ever had.

Nate's Belief

"I'm sorry to have to tell you" April sighed as she swept a lock of her dirty blond hair over her ear. She usually wore it in a tight bun to avoid the annoyance. She lifted the teacup off the counter and handed it to Diana who was sitting on the white couch. "I swear I didn't do anything to lead him on. I was just in shock!" She sat down in the matching white chair beside the church closest to Diana and crossed her trouser clad legs.

Diana stared at the floor for a moment. Her long black hair cascading around her face. She finally lifted her head and swept her hair back with her free hand so she could take a sip. She set the cup down before clenching her eyes shut as she sat back on the couch. Her short flared skirt spread on either side of her "I know you didn't" she said quietly, before exclaiming "FUCK!"

April reached across from her chair and put her hand on Diana's knee. "I'm sorry".

Diana shook her head. "I'm a fucking idiot!" She bit her lip. "Rachel told me Nate hit on her and I called her a bitch!" She leaned forward again. She felt sick. "She was trying to do the right thing and I threw it in her face. FUCK!" She clutched her belly. "How many women is he sleeping with that didn't try to warn me?"

"I don't know," April replied.

"What happened?" Diana asked.

April looked up at the mantle as she began to tell her story. "You know, how I put the call out for research volunteers last week? Well Nate showed up. Like everyone else, I handed him a questionnaire and took his medical history. All that seemed to meet criteria so I gave him a tour of the lab."

"..and that was when he hit on you?" Diana asked.

"In the mapping room." April said. "We have the emission tunnel and the exam table all set up with the soft restraints so we can stay on—target. He made a joke about the restraints being kinky. Honestly it's the same joke almost everyone makes when they see the table. I just explained that they were necessary to ensure our equipment was focused on the intended portion of the brain for proper mapping. The technical details are pretty dull so I just give the elevator pitch,after which most people move on."

"But not Nate?" Diana asked.

April shook her head. "With the wrist cuff still in his hand he said 'if I'm in the study, there would be no reason for Diana to question the time we spent in here. Why don't we take turns being strapped down and playing doctor?"

"Really?" Diana exclaimed, appalled.

"Not only is he a cheater, but his lines are fucking awful!" April agreed.

"Fucking ASSHOLE" Diana cried out. "I'm dumping his ass tonight! I just wish I could kick him in the balls first!" She took a deep breath "Fuck it! I'm kicking him in the balls and THEN dumping him!"

"Wait" April said. A smile began to stretch across

her face. “Do you really want to get him?”
Diana’s fury was paused by curiosity. “Yes?” She said April's facial expression was a little creepy.
“Don’t dump him. Don’t kick him, Don’t let him know that you know.” April said. She paused as if reconsidering something. “Yes.” She said to herself “I have something infinitely worse in mind.”
“What are you talking about?” Diana asked.
“My research.” April explained. “He already signed the consents and a waiver. I’m going to admit him into the study.” She burst out laughing.
“What?” Diana asked
“The Gamma-scan emitter, we have to be very careful when we use it to map the brain because if it’s tuned wrong it can cause brain damage”. April said.
“You are not lobotomizing him!” Diana cried out.
“Oh no, not like that.” April reassured. “But, if I tune it just right, focused on just the right part of the brain at a very specific frequency, while I state a simple suggestion, he will accept the statement as absolute unshakable truth that he will cling to no matter how much contradictory evidence is put in front of him or how much it costs. We call it a “Faith Cascade”.
“I don’t know,” Diana said. “What would we make him believe?”
“I have a few ideas, but, in reality, anything we want.”
Diana watched the fire in the fireplace for a few minutes as the two women sat in silence.

Suddenly her eyes went wide. "Oh, God! I have the perfect belief!"

April pulled the strap tight on Nate's left wrist. The rest of him was secured firmly to the table. "Comfy?" She asked.
"Yeah..." he replied. "Though you could make me feel a lot better."
April smiled down at him as she trailed her finger from his bound wrist, across his waist and down. She could feel his cock straining against the denim of his jeans, she trailed down to the tip, to his thigh and then turned away. "Maybe later" she said as she cast a look at the 1 way glass where she knew Diana was sitting and watching. She selected the new head-cage that was euphemistically called a net. It was a steel mesh stretched to match the subject's face perfectly. She put it down over Nate's head and locked it in place, preventing him from speaking or moving his head at all. "This will make sure we don't accidentally fry your brain," April explained.
She saw Nate's eyes boggle.
"That's just a joke. We are mapping at such a low power that you should be fine, this is so you don't move and get us lost". She reassured him before sliding the platform he was fastened to down so that the Scan-Tube enveloped his head down to his shoulders.
"Nate, I am going to the next room where I will talk to you through the speakers. I'll ask you a series of

questions and you just need to think of the answer not say them. Thumbs up if you are Okay. If you need to be let out, smack the table with your palm 3 times. Got it?"

Nate put a thumb up.

"Okay!" April said in a cheery voice. "I'll see you on the other side!"

She opened the door to the darkened control room and stepped inside. Diana was there, illuminated in the blue green glow of the monitors with a bemused smirk on her face.

"Cop a little feel?" She asked with a giggle.

"It put him at ease." April replied.

"That's not what it looked like," Said Diana with a grin. "He looked like he was going to bust his fly wide open. For all his faults, he does have an impressive cock.

"For now." April replied. "Let's get started."

April turned the system on for a standard scan and waited for the signal. "Okay Nate, we are going to ask you some questions and you are going to think of the answer. The machine will map the thoughts and help us determine the structure of thought."

On the table Nate put his thumb up. On the computer monitor an area along his motor cortex lit up.

"Let's get started." She flipped open a binder. "On a cloudless day what color is the sky?"

The computer monitor indicated a pattern on the brain.

"That's consistent with what we read for 'blue,'"

April explained to Diana.

"What color is grass?"

The screen highlighted another pattern.

"Is ice hot, or cold? Is night bright or dark? Sugar is bitter, true or false? What is larger, a mouse or an elephant?...." April continued on through several pages while the computer recorded each result. After she had gone through half the binder, she shot a grin to Diana and clicked an icon on her screen. The scanner changed pitch slightly and a warning box appeared on the screen. April clicked it away and leaned into the microphone. "Following Diana's advice is the key to your eventual happiness." Another warning box appeared.

WARNING: FAITH CASCADE DETECTED!

April smiled and pointed to the alert.

Diana nodded in approval.

April clicked another icon and the machine pitch returned to normal while the screen indicated that the session logs were being deleted.

"Nate, we had a calibration adjustment. We will start again in a moment." April said into the microphone.

Nate held up his thumb.

"How was April's study?" Diana innocently asked as Nate came into the apartment.

"Dull!" Nate said. "She just strapped me to a table and asked a bunch of questions while her machine picked my brain." Nate hung up his jacket and vaulted over the couch landing next to her. He put his hand on her thigh and licked his lips. “I couldn’t wait to get home to you.”

Diana looked at him for a moment. “Horny?” She asked.

Nate reached over with his right hand and cupped Diana’s beast. “Oh you know it.”

Diana grabbed his wrist gently and moved it away. “Sex is better when you’re horny, isn’t it?”

Nate slid his hand up her thigh, she could feel his finger against her labia. “Oh yeah”.

“So.” Diana said. “You should lean into that. If it's good when you’re horny, you should see what it’s like when you’re really horny!”

“I should…” Nate agreed.

“You should avoid cumming for a week.” Diana said flatly.

“Oh wow, you think I should?” Nate asked.

“In fact, you should wear a chastity cage to keep your cock from getting hard.” She added. “I bought you one. It’s in the bathroom. You should put it on and bring me the key.”

Nate sighed, his disappointment visible and Diana worried that she had pushed too hard. He then got to his feet and went into the bathroom.

Diana knew she had him.

A few minutes later, Nate emerged with a sour look. “I was already hard, so it was almost impossible to bend into the thing! If I had jacked off, it would have been easier, but you think I shouldn’t so I just had to jam it. It hurts like hell!”

He handed the small key to Diana who slipped it onto a chain and clipped it around her neck.

She looked at his jeans and could see the faint outline of the metal rails. "Looks like it's pretty cramped in there." She said,

"You have no idea," Nate replied.

"You will probably be more comfortable in skirts," Diana said simply.

"Skirts?" Nate said. "You think?"

"Oh absolutely!" Diana replied.

"I'll need to order some."

"You would be surprised how stretchy they can be." Diana got to her feet. "Let me see if I have anything that might fit you. Take those Jeans off while you wait." She heard a zipper behind her and smiled to herself as she passed into the bedroom. She took out her phone and pulled up a chat with April.

Diana: Cucked, caged, and about to be skirted

April: Enjoy your sissy bimbo

Diana: I'm just getting started!

Diana reached into her closet and pulled out a short skater skirt that was among the outfits she had already picked up for Nate. She also grabbed a pair of pink lacy panties and returned to the main room.

Nate was standing in his white briefs.

"No." Diana said. "That won't do at all."

"What?" Nate asked.

"For one, this skirt is short and no one wants to see ugly tightly-whites under a pretty skirt." She said,

"Funny, but, I'm a dude!" Nate replied.

Diana realized that she hadn't worded it as advice. "I just think you should wear the appropriate underwear to the clothing over it. Guy-clothes get guy-underwear, girly clothes should go with girly underwear." She held up the panties.

Nate made to argue and then stopped. "If you think so."

A few moments later, Nate was standing in their living room caged, wearing pretty pink panties under his black skater's skirt.

"Almost right," Diana said.

"Now what?" Nate moaned. "I hate this!"

"As you should," Diana said. "You should always remember that you are a man inside, no matter how girly you get."

"Yeah!" Nate replied. "Just cause I'm in panties and a skirt, I'm still Nate!"

"Hmm" Diana pondered. "You know, in panties and a skirt, you should probably use a girly name."

Nate's eyes went wide. He had just affirmed that he was still a man and that he hated being girly, but he also knew that Diana was right. As much conflict as Nate felt, he knew that her advice would make him happiest. He couldn't seem to get enough air. "What name?" He finally asked.

"Don't know." Diana said. "You should think about it while you shave your legs."

"I wasn't...." Nate began.

"You would look better in your pretty skirt with bare legs. You should shave them every day." Diana interrupted.

Nate's shoulders slumped. He stalked off to the bathroom where Diana had conveniently left all the supplies he would need for him.

While Nate wrestled with the razor, Diana called through the door. "You should do your whole body and face too!" While she opened up her laptop and began writing a personal ad. When she reached the bottom she called into the bathroom. "Pick a name yet?"

"What about Natalie?" Nate replied.

"You should always go by Natalie! She/Her" Diana replied cheerily. She signed the personal ad "Natalie"

"Here" Diana said as she entered the bathroom. Natalie was shaving her chest. Diana could see her cock cage with nothing but bare skin around it. She set out 2 massive silicone breast forms with adhesives and a black bra. "Once you finish, you should use the bra to figure where they should sit and then glue them on. When we go out tonight, you would look pretty silly in a skirt without tits." She then set a glittery crop-top next to it. "You should show off your abs." Then she opened her makeup bag. "After you are dressed, you better let me show you how to do your face."

"Okay." Natalie said, defeated. "But I don't want to go out like this"

"You're caged for a week!" Diana replied. "That means skirts and everything that comes with it all week. You should get used to being seen as a girl.

Even though you should always hate it." Diana enjoyed twisting the knife a little.
"What about work!? I can't teach a class like this!" Natalie exclaimed in a panic.
Diana sighed. "The University has a strict non-discrimination policy that includes gender identity. Tomorrow morning, you ought to go to administration and register as transgender. Tell them that you are transitioning and they won't be able to fire you." Natalie's eyes went wide. "I guess that would work." She thought she could see a small tear in the corner of Natalie's eye before she left.

Like every night for the past week, Diana walked into Nate's favorite bar and held the door open for Natalie, formerly Nate the tough history professor and now the laughingstock of the campus.
Natalie carefully stepped one foot in front of the other, heel to toe on her 3" black heels at the end of her fishnet thigh-high stocking clad legs, each one topped with a purple bow on the front that matched the color of the interior of her black mini skater skirt. Every quick movement or slight breeze was enough to swish the thin fabric enough to reveal Natalie's lacy panties encasing her visibly caged cock. Her midriff was bare beneath her shimmery black top. She wore a black and silver dog-collar with a tag that said "sissy" on it.
Her makeup was full glam, Diana had suggested she clean and reapply several times a day to keep

it fresh. Glossy red lips, blue to pink eyeshadow and blush, though her cheeks were already red with embarrassment as she looked out through her artificial lashes, at the gathering of Nate's old friends from campus who now came nightly just to see what Natalie had become and what wig she would wear. Tonight she wore a pink bob-cut not much longer than what Nate had at the beginning of the week decorated with black ribbons to match her dog-collar and outfit. Each night was more humiliating than the night before, and walking in was the worst moment of the night, so this was the newest worst moment of Natalies life. Still, deep down, she knew Diana's advice would pay off in the end and happiness lay on the other side of this. She followed Diana to the bar, and tried to smooth her skirt under her ass before sitting on the stool, but it was too short and her thong-split bare cheeks planted on the wood, pressing the buttplug in deeper. Diana has suggested she wear a plug 24/7 to enhance her horniness through the week, and the ones she provided Natalie with got bigger and bigger as the week went on. Now, she felt like she was being split as she rested on the stool.

Natalie eyed the bottles of Irish Whiskey Nate preferred but ordered the Chardonnay that Diana suggested she drink to "keep in character." Just a few more hours, she thought. The week was over and Diana had promised that Natalie would be let out of her cage and have sex tonight.

The night out passed without confrontation

thankfully, though Natalie saw that her students had now joined the gawkers who didn't even pretend not to stare at her over their drinks.

Ashley, one of Natalie's more attractive students who Nate had taken to bed a few times came over. Diana had mentioned a foursome tonight, maybe Ashley was going to be one of the participants! Natalie could feel her cock straining to straighten against the harsh steel cage.

"Professor...uh...Natalie?" Ashley ventured. "I had almost convinced myself that you were just a predator and a bastard." She reached into her purse and pulled out a woven cotton blue, pink, and white bracelet. She took Natalie's hand and tied it around her wrist. "But now I see that you were just trying to model the toxic male stereotype the patriarchy pushed on you. I'm so proud of you and how brave you are being, to show us all your truth." She leaned in and kissed Natalie on the cheek. "Welcome sister." She smiled and walked away.

Natalie watched her go, and then looked down at the Trans-flag she now wore on her wrist.

"That was sweet," Diana said. "You should never take it off."

Natalie looked down and nodded in agreement trying to figure out how to explain it once she was Nate again tomorrow.

"You should pay our tab," Diana said. "It's almost time!"

Natalie obediently paid for the drinks and followed

Diana out to the car.

Natalie was surprised when Diana parked on campus rather than back at the apartment. "Are you ready for the most intense sexual experience of your life?" she asked as she climbed out of the driver's seat.

Natalie opened her door and had just put her heels on the pavement when Diana came around and clipped a leash to her dog collar. "You should heel girl!" She said,

Natalie's heart was racing as she followed at the end of her leash while Diana led her down a path through some bushes and into one of the campus' isolated grottos. She turned to Natalie and held up the key. "Let's get you unlocked!"

Natalie smiled wide as Diana knelt in front of her and she could feel the cage open. As soon as she was free, she felt her cock stand at full mast and a trickle of precum dribble out. She was about to burst, she had never felt so horny! Diana had been right. Natalie's faith had paid off!

"You should get on your hands and knees." Diana said. "I'll get your plug out."

Natalie had been taking her own plugs out all week, there was something sexy about having Diana do it, she eagerly got down and pushed her pantied butt up in the air.

Diana clicked a lock onto Natalie's leash and then locked the other side to a garden fence in front of her before moving behind Natalie.

Natalie stared at the chain in disbelief as she felt Diana pull her thong down her legs and then the sensation of the plug being pulled slowly and gently from her ass. "Good, now you're ready. The boys will be here soon." Diana said.

"Boys!?" Natalie exclaimed in surprise. "I'm not fucking boys!"

"Of course not!" Diana replied. "Girls get fucked by boys!"

"I'm not a girl!" Natalie protested.

"You should look at how you're dressed, how you spent your week, and the paperwork you have done for work and recognize that you are a girl," Diana countered.

Natalie's breath quivered as her absolute faith crashed into her sense of identity. Diana dug deeper. "And since you are a girl, you should let the boys fuck you. You should always let boys have what they want from you."

"Oh God." Natalie muttered. "I...I...guess I will."

"Good girl," Diana said.

"Do I have to be chained up like this?" She asked.

"Yes, I don't want you wandering off." Diana replied.

"I'm nervous Diana." Natalie's voice cracked.

"Don't be. Once your lovers turn up one by one to break you in, you won't be nervous anymore." She smiled down at her victim.

"L-lovers...?" Natalie whimpered.

"Don't act surprised my cute boyfriend. I can see you're excited." Diana pointed to the tented rise in

Natalie's skirt.

"I can't....I just...." Natalie whimpered. "I thought...".

"Oh, no." Natalie replied. "You should never use that thing for sex again. But don't worry. If you relax while they are in your boy-pussy, they may hit that special spot and give you an orgasm too."

"Relax..." Natalie repeated to herself.

They could hear men's voices and shuffling in the bushes behind Natalie.

"I was surprised at how many responded to your personal ad." Diana said.

"Personal ad?" Natalie replied.

"I posted it at the beginning of the week under casual encounters". Diana grinned wide. "Here she is, boys! Form a line!" She announced.

Natalie looked over her shoulder and recognized a student Nate had failed last semester at the front of the line already unzipping his fly. She gulped, but knew she should let the boys have what they wanted.

As she felt the first thrust of a cock slide into her lubed anus, Diana got down on one knee.

"Since you told your office you were transitioning, and boys like real pussies more than boy-pussies, you should go through with it and fully transition, hormones, voice, face surgery, implants and bottom surgery. You should turn yourself into a living love-doll so the boys can have what they always wanted." She kissed Natalie on the ear. "Also, since you're a girl now, you can't be my boyfriend. I'm keeping the apartment, but Jeff and Stan who are a few back in line have a spare room you can have in exchange for daily blow-jobs. You should accept the offer."

Natalie just nodded. She could feel hot cum leaking out of her and barely had time to catch her breath before the next boy pushed into her.

"One more thing." Diana said. "You should never forget that deep down you are a man and you will always hate being a girl and being used by men. You should never let that go, but you should never let that stop you from being the sluttiest little fuck-toy these boys have ever seen. Got that?" She asked.

Natalie moaned and nodded. To her shame, she could feel her own cock pulsing and felt the spurt as she came from being fucked by a man.

"I'll leave you with the boys now," Diana said. "But you know where I live. You should never hesitate to come to me when you need advice." She kissed Natalie one last time on her sweating forehead and stood up. "Boys!" She called. "Her mouth is free too!"

As Dian walked out of the grotto, she could hear a "Gluck,Gluck, Gluck" sound coming from Natalie as she learned what it was to be finger-cuffs.

No Trespassing

1, Marcus

It was more of a flier than a sign. Printed on common paper and stapled to the tree beside the gate. Bruce pulled it down as he slipped the locked chain up over a wooden post and then swung the rusty arm aside, waving the truck in. He was a tall and broad-shouldered man with the beginnings of a beard growing on his chin and red hair combed straight back.

As the driver pulled alongside, Bruce said, "Turn the headlights off!"

"I won't be able to see a damn thing!" Marcus protested as he squinted through his thick-rimmed glasses at the darkness around them.

"Nah, it's fine!" Bruce reassured him. "I'll walk in front down the middle of the lane with this glow stick, just follow me!"

Marcus ground his teeth. "Why here? We're supposed to bring back a statue for the campus fountain! I don't see anything in these woods!"

"Gargoyles," Bruce responded. "The main house has Gargoyles. God knows why. A Victorian in the middle of the forest is weird enough!"

"Gargoyles?" Stacy asked. "What's so great about Gargoyles?"

"Halloween touch!" Bruce said. "Benny and Jason are stealing the General off the plinth tonight. Haha, the statue gone! Big deal, no one cares." He shrugged. "But we REPLACE the General with a stone Gargoyle, suddenly it's a magic trick! We transformed the old coot into a monster!"

"Gargoyles? Plural?" Marcus asked.

Bruce nodded. "We'll only take one, but there are a couple to choose from."

Marcus sighed and reached down to shut the lights off.

"Are you sure no one will be there?" Stacy asked from the passenger seat. She was dressed conservatively as usual with a button-down blouse and long skirt.

Bruce flashed a devilish grin at her. "No one lives here and the owners are handing out candy to all the little kiddies! I know this property better than they do. Trust me, princess!"

"Oh wait, is this the camp?" Marcus asked.

"The one and same," Bruce replied. He swung the gate closed behind the truck and slipped the chain back into place. He came up to the passenger side, "This house has a special place in my heart! When the council had to sell it a lot of people were pissed! Thank God the guy who bought it just uses it for hunting and camping or we would have another riverside development on our hands," he said to Stacy as he passed to begin walking down the lane in front of them. Stacy shook her head, waving her tight ponytail behind her in frustration.

Though she lived on campus, her family was from one of the nicer riverside developments in the county. There was no illusion that Bruce didn't intend that as a comment on her. Bruce's family had lived in the area for centuries and didn't approve of the recent invasion of suburbia to their rural oasis.

Marcus did his best to keep the truck centered on Bruce as they made their way down the dirt lane.

"What's he mean by that?" Kelly asked from the back seat. She was wearing a loose tank top over a very visible black sports bra with spandex leggings.

Marcus shrugged. "This is where Bruce lost his V-Card."

"Wait, wasn't this a scout camp?" Kelly said in surprise.

"EWWW!" Stacy exclaimed. "It wasn't with a counselor was it?"

Marcus laughed. "Kinda!"

"Oh my God!" Kelly sat back in her seat hard.

"Not like that." Marcus reassured her. "This camp was for boys and girls, opposite sides of the property. Bruce went here since he was eight." Marcus squinted through the windshield, "When Bruce aged out, he stayed with the program as a camp leader for one summer. There was this counselor from the girls camp that Bruce got along with." The tuck bounced over something unseen. "The house was in the middle between the camps so Bruce and her would meet there."

"Kinda romantic," Stacy sighed. She loved to read about secret lovers in forbidden rendezvous.

Marcus cocked his head, "Romantic is not how Bruce describes it."

"How does he describe it?" Kelly asked. She was now sitting forward between the seats.

"Some of the dirtiest sex seen this side of the dirt! Is how he described it," Marcus said.

"Boys!" Kelly exclaimed and sat back.

"What?" Marcus asked. "That's what he said! Said she was still number one in his spank-bank."

"What's a spank-bank?" Stacy asked.

"Oh no! Honey." Kelly exclaimed and put her hand on Stacy's shoulder. "You lucky sheltered thing!"

"You know!" Marcus said. "The fantasy file. What you think about when you....please yourself."

"Oooohhhh!" Stacy said. "Ewww!"

"Seriously?" Marcus asked. "You don't have a spank–bank?"

"Women have fantasies." Kelly cut in. "But we don't refer to them in that way!"

"Is there a difference?" Marcus demanded.

Kelly went to open her mouth and stopped.

Stacy just looked doe eyed between them. "Firemen!" she blurted. "I like firemen!"

Both of them stared at her in disbelief until the truck started to rumble on underbrush and Marcus was forced to pay attention to Bruce's glow stick again.

"Like them." Kelly said. "But did you ever....."

"Ever flick the bean to em?" Marcus asked, "Stirred

the soup?"

"Oh my GOD!" Kelly complained. "You are so gross!"

"Hey, our terms are just as bad!" Marcus said. "Choke the Chicken, Pull Peter, Rub one Out... though I guess you girls could use that phrase too."

"That's not the point!" Kelly said.

"Check the oil," Stacy said to everyone's surprise.

Marcus slammed on the brakes and burst out laughing.

"STACY!" Kelly said before she started laughing.

Stacy blushed. "It's just one I heard somewhere," she said sheepishly as her friends fought to regain their composure.

"What's going on!" Bruce demanded, having come back to the driver-side window.

"Stacy was just telling us how she checks her oil!" Marcus said before laughing again.

Bruce's brow furrowed and then his eyes widened. "WHAT?"

"We were talking about your camp counselor liaisons!" Kelly interjected.

"And your spank bank," Marcus added.

Bruce glowered at him. "Ok, cheerleader chaser!"

"HEY!" Marcus barked.

Bruce looked past him at the two girls. "Markie's spank bank, all pom-poms and short skirts!" He looked back at his friend disapprovingly. "Get some imagination man!"

"Just guide the truck!" Marcus growled.

"Sure thing buddy." Bruce smiled then as he

walked away then started waving his glow stick around. “Give me a D. R. I. V. E, What's it spell! DRIVE!”

Marcus worked his jaw for a moment. “So what’s yours Kelly?”

“Oh no!” the blond replied. “I’m staying out of this one!”

“No fair!” Stacy cried.

“Agreed.” Marcus added. “We all spilled ours, what gets you wet?”

“Well,” Kelly paused. “Lifeguards.” she admitted. “And I know it’s cliche and kind of weird since that’s my job every summer but, it’s always been hot guys in red trunks.”

“Can I change mine?” Stacy teased.

“We’re here!” Bruce announced.

At the end of the long dark tree-lined dirt lane, the road turned to the right and the sky opened above it. They were now driving across a clearing, the moonlight giving everything a silver hue as Marcus pulled past Bruce and stopped just long enough for his friend to jump into the truck bed. Bruce stood behind the cab and smacked the truck’s roof 2 times.

Ahead the house loomed, lit from behind by moonlight it was a massive featureless shape before them.

“This is it!” Marcus announced as he stopped the truck and put it into park.

Bruce jumped down. “The Gargoyles are on the roofline. We should be able to get to them from the

3rd floor windows!"
"Getting to them isn't what worries me," Marcus said. "Getting them back down is going to be the tough part! We should have brought a couple more guys!"
"Sexist!" Kelly objected. "I'm in a hell of a lot better shape than you computer-boy!" She pushed past the two men and climbed the wooden steps of the Victorian house, halting on the front porch to turn to her three friends. "Are we doing this or not?"
Bruce smiled, "Oh, we're doing this, just not through that door. It's locked."
Kelly turned the knob, it didn't budge.
"So what's the plan?" she asked.
"Follow me." Bruce led the group around the back to the cellar doors set in the ground at an angle. A chain ran between the handles but Bruce had done this before, one handle was not connected at the bottom and he was able to lift it far enough to slip the chain out from under it. He pulled the door up and open, and passed out small flashlights he had in his pocket. "Be prepared." he smiled as he handed the last light to Stacy.
She averted her eyes but smiled back.
Once all of them were down the stairs he pulled the door shut behind them and pushed past them. "Wait here," he said as he disappeared behind a shelf filled with jars. A few moments later they heard a loud <CLICK> and several bare lightbulbs hanging from the unfinished rafters lit up.
"GREAT!" Bruce exclaimed. "They never bothered

to turn off the power!"

Stacy looked nervous. "Uh, won't people see the light?"

"Remember the drive from the gate?" Marcus asked. "There are 500 yards of forest between us and any roads! We could throw a rave and no one would know!"

"Then why did we drive in with the lights off?" Kelly asked.

Marcus paused. "Yeah, Bruce! I understand the first hundred yards, but after that..."

"It's more spooky that way!" Bruce grinned. "Besides, I wanted to make sure no one was camping, had to look for campfires and keep my nose open."

"I thought you said no one goes camping on Halloween!" Marcus accused.

"Almost!" Bruce allowed. "Almost no one goes camping on Halloween!" He was looking around the cellar like he was confused. "Except for me," he added under his breath.

"Uh, Bruce? Is something wrong?" Kelly asked.

Bruce pulled a jar off one of the shelves and stared at the top in disbelief. "Applebutter by Idun." he muttered. He put the jar on the shelf. "Last time I was down here, this place was a dump." He walked over to a wall and traced his hand across it. "Janice and I scratched our initials in the concrete right here!" The wall was bare and smooth. He pointed to the shelves filled with jars. "And those shelves were broken with nothing on them!"

"Do you think someone is here?" Marcus asked.
Bruce shook his head. "No, the power would be on if there was."

2, Bruce

A merry voice broke in from across the cellar. "Unless someone prefers it off!" There was a loud crack and the basement was cast into total darkness once again!

Stacy screamed.

Marcus shouted, "WHAT THE FUCK?!"

Kelly backed up against the wall breathing heavily.

Bruce moved to the stairs out of the cellar while he fished in his pocket for his flashlight. He tripped in the darkness and fell onto the steps. "I can't find my flashlight guys!" he called into the darkness. "Someone light theirs!"

There was a pause. "Mine is gone too!" Marcus called but it seemed like he was across the room.

"Kelly?" Bruce cried.

"Bruce?" she called back faintly from the distance. "Where did you go? I can't see anything!"

"Stacy?" Bruce heard a faint voice in the distance but couldn't make out any words.

"All alone! All Alone!" the strange merry voice seemed to be laughing in Bruce's ear. He swung in that direction and his hand struck the staircase wall, throbbing in pain. "Oh no! No one there!" the voice mocked. "No one to strike, but someone to fear!"

"Who are you?" Bruce cried out.

"No No!" the voice responded. "Names are precious things and precious things have power! Why do you give away so many precious things in this cellar? Your name, Bruce, the names of your friends, even your virtue to Janice! I watched! I listened! I learned as you gave them all away! I took your treasure and that of so many others and I hoarded them here for me alone! I thought I was alone now, but here you are! What fun!" The voice seemed to be dancing around Bruce's head as it spoke. "Halloween!" it scoffed. "A mockery of what it was but I can play along!" The voice now seemed to loom over Bruce. "A treat perhaps?"

Bruce's body seemed to shiver as every part of him felt intense pleasure. He could feel things he never imagined before and he gasped. As he breathed in, his chest expanded. As he pulled his legs up to his stomach they reshaped. He felt the throb of approaching climax and squeezed his muscles trying to hold back. His balls rose when he did so but kept going! He felt them pull up inside him and as the climax overcame his efforts he felt each pulse of his ejaculation erupt from a smaller and smaller source. He screamed and a high-pitched voice came from his throat.

"Or is it a trick?" the voice taunted.

Bruce grabbed his throat and his hand felt too thin and small as it grasped the smooth bare skin of his neck. He rubbed it across his chin and face. His beard was gone! His hand went to a mane of wavy hair that fell around his ears and he pulled at it to see if it was real. His socks seemed to crawl up his legs while his boots retreated down to his ankles while his khaki pants shredded and reformed. At last, the sensations ceased and the lights came on. Bruce looked down in shock. A pair of large breasts were clearly under the white blouse with the peter pan collar she wore. She had a dark blue vest with a number of patches and emblems sewn to it. Under that, she wore a pleated khaki skirt with socks pulled up above her knees and white tennis shoes.

She ran her hands over her newly transformed body. It was a body Bruce knew almost as well as her own. "I'm Janice," she muttered.

"A treat for you all that is also a trick! You will get to live out your fantasies firsthand as you become what you desire!" The voice laughed and swirled around Bruce as she turned and ran up the stairs to the door outside.

Just as she was about to push it open the voice said, "Leave my house without finishing the game and you can stay as you are forever!"

Bruce halted. She looked down at her breasts, felt the strap of her bra around her ribs, and felt the lack between her legs. She turned around to face the empty cellar. "What game?" she asked.

"Ahhh." the voice said. "The boy asks who, the girl asks what! Neither listens as I have already said."

"Please!" Bruce asked. "I can't be a girl! What do I

need to do to change back!"
"She doesn't like her treat!" the voice sounded hurt. "None of them seem to but that will change! Find one another and live out your lust! Once that is done I will answer your question!"
Bruce's manicured hand drifted down and pressed against her flat crotch through her skirt. "Live out our lust? You mean I have to..." she curled her fingers and felt them press against her pussy. "Oh God!" she moaned.
"Before the sun rises, for then my power fades, a year you will have to wait to call on me again! So hurry girl, find a mate and spread those legs or keep what's between them for a year at the least!"
Bruce ran deeper into the cellar. "Kelly! Stacy! Marcus?" she called. Her high-pitched voice was like nails on a chalkboard to her own ears.
"Here!" came a girl's voice, though it sounded far away.
Bruce followed the sound and found herself at the foot of a staircase that climbed to a closed door. She looked back, she remembered the stairs into the house being on the other side of the cellar, but then again, she remembered having a cock when she came into the cellar so this is all relative. She ran up the stairs and pushed the door open to find herself standing in the library. She scanned the room and saw a black shape standing in the shadows.
"Hello?" she called to the shape.
"Who are you?" said the same girl's voice Bruce had

heard downstairs. The voice was a little raspy and very sexy.

"My name is..." she looked down at her boobs and then back at the shape. "Bruce."

"Oh My God!" The shape tottered forward trying not to fall. She had straight dark black hair with purple ends running down to her waist. She wore black lipstick and winged eyeliner on a round pale face over a black spiked dog collar. A webbing of straps over her shoulders disappeared under a shiny black corset that pushed her massive breasts up to make two globes on her chest. She had a pleated black miniskirt wider than it was long that revealed her black panties and the garter straps holding up her black fishnet stockings that disappeared into a pair of black platform heels. "I'm Marcus." she said.

"Marcus?" Bruce said. "But you're..."

"I know!" Marcus replied, "And you're Janice!"

"The voice!" Bruce said.

"I heard it too," Marcus replied. "Giving us our fantasies." She gestured down at herself.

"You always said you were into cheerleaders!" Bruce accused.

The girl shrugged causing her breasts to bounce a little despite the constraining garment. "I lied," she looked down. "It's always been big-titty goth chicks."

"I can see that!" Bruce said. "But why lie about it?"

Marcus slumped into a chair with her legs wide open. She realized immediately that she was flashing her black silk panties and slapped her legs together, pulling down the hem of her skirt but it was too short to cover her crotch. "I get enough crap about the tabletop games. Nerdy gamer into goth chicks is such a cliche. I just wanted to break the mold a little." she sighed and looked down at her own breasts. "Fuuuuuuck."

"We've gotta..." Bruce said.

"What?" Marcus looked up. "You mean the voice? Yeah, it said we had to fuck to get our bodies back!"

"So what are we waiting for?" Bruce asked as she stepped forward. "You're a hot chick, I'm a hot chick, I can feel myself getting... it's weird."

"Wet?" Marcus asked.

"Yeah. Wet, and a hardon in my tits." Bruce put her hand on Marcus' shoulder and traced it to her collar. "So let's get this over with and get our bodies back!" She hooked her finger through the loop in Marcus' collar and pulled her up to her feet. She was a little taller than Bruce now, Bruce pulled her in and kissed her. Marcus' hands went to Bruce's ass and gripped tight. Bruce's eyes went wide as she felt her crotch warm while Marcus squeezed. Marcus' hands went to Bruce's hips and pushed her back for a moment.

"Wait! Isn't this gay?" Marcus asked.

"Two chicks who used to be guys fucking to get our dicks back?" Bruce asked. "If you can untangle that knot, you're smarter than me. Who cares?" she slid her hand under Marcus' skirt and pushed her panties aside. Marcus was completely bald under her panties just as Bruce was sure she was too. They were fantasy women after all. Her finger slipped between Marcus' lips and found the nub she was looking for.

"OH HOLY SHIT!" Marcus exclaimed as Bruce started rubbing. She froze and slowly descended as her knees seemed to collapse in slow motion. "You..Have..No..Idea!" she gasped before looking down and shooting a grin at Bruce. She lifted Bruce's skirt and pulled her white lace panties down to her thighs before pushing her own fingers into Bruce's slit.

In moments they were both kneeling on the floor as they fingered each other and kissed. Marcus pushed her middle and ring fingers up inside Bruce and she almost choked at the sensation of being penetrated for the first time. She could feel Marcus' fingers inside her and her brain didn't want to process it. The sensations as her fingers massaged her insides made her eyes cross as she plunged her own fingers into Marcus who moaned loudly as she entered. The sensations grew and seemed to echo off her hips and up into her stomach with a growing tension that suddenly broke! Bruce tried to scream through her first climax as a woman but no sound came from her voice. At last, she gasped as the waves seemed to roll back only to feel them building again. She redoubled her efforts with her own hand and Marcus let out a growling grunt as she came. Marcus moved her left hand down from Bruce's hip and pressed her thumb into Bruce's clit while she continued to finger fuck her with her right. Bruce rolled her eyes back as the second, and then the third climax washed over her and then another and then another. They were both on their sides, their fingers still buried in each other when Bruce was aware of her surroundings again. She pulled her fingers back and pushed Marcus onto her back, then pulled her black silk panties down. She licked her lips and then tasted her friend's pussy. Marcus sounded like she was crying after the third orgasm and Bruce came up to check on her, pausing to rub her soaked face on Marcus' bulging cleavage. Marcus just pushed Bruce around onto her back, climbed on top, lifted Bruce's skirt and returned the favor.

Bruce stared at the ceiling as Marcus' tongue gave her sensations she never knew existed. At last, a massive wave, larger than any she had already experienced broke and she finally cried out in a feminine squeak as she experienced the biggest orgasm of her life.

"That's the spirit!" the voice said as Marcus raised her wet face to look up at Bruce.

3, Kelly

This was all so weird! Kelly's mind tried to comprehend the sensations it was receiving as he moved a large hand over bulging pectoral muscles, down washboard abs, and found the hardening protrusion that was tenting the red swim trunks he was wearing. "I'm a dude!" he muttered as he tried to push the hard on down with painful results. "What the fuck!" he said and he grabbed his throat, feeling the hard lump of his adam's apple in shock. He was barefoot, though the soles of his feet were so thick that it felt like he was wearing sandals. He picked one up and ran a thumb across the dry rough surface and then drew his hand up his hairy muscled leg. "Un-fucking-believable!" His hand went up the leg of his shorts to the rock hard cock under his trunks. He wrapped his hand around it and again tried to bend it. "Ow! Nope!" he said and managed to keep it straight while pointing it down a leg of the swim trunks. His fingertips brushed his balls and he saw the leg of the trunks bounce up as his cock took notice. "Jesus!" he grumbled and suddenly realized how aggressive his voice was now with its deeper tone. "Wow! AAAoooooooooo!" He played with the pitch of his voice for a second.

He had heard the voice's taunts as he had been transformed in the dark. Breasts becoming pecs and clit growing into dick while spandex retreated and reshaped into the baggy red trunks he now wore that said "GUARD" on the leg. He was the embodiment of his own sexual fantasy. Ronnie Pope. The pool manager of Kelly's community pool for those magical summers in her early teens. The guard Kelly still thought of when she slid forward while the bathtub was filling.

The cock pushed up past the mesh and fabric that hardly gave any resistance as it slid by and Kelly's trunks were once again tented in front. "I've gotta get rid of this thing!" he muttered as he began searching the cellar for anyone else.

He was initially surprised that he could see over the top of the shelves that lined the cellar. He was beginning to appreciate the height when he turned and banged his forehead into an air duct. Shaking the cobwebs loose, he began down an aisle between two shelves and banged a shoulder into one of them. "Goddamnit!" he muttered, "Im a fucking giant!"

The voice had said he would have to act out his fantasy with this body. That meant sex, and that meant a partner. Kelly hated to think of what that would feel like in this behemoth, but if that's what it took to get back to normal size and get rid of this sausage, then so be it!

The stairs were back by the electrical panel. He

began climbing them, hearing the creak of the wood under his feet and wondering how much he weighed. He pushed open the door to find himself standing in a small kitchen. On the counter was a fruit basket filled with dozens of apples of various varieties, yellow, red, green and orange.

There was an open cookie jar filled with oatmeal raisin cookies and the smell of cinnamon filled the room. Hanging over the door was a wreath of mistletoe. "Wrong holiday!" Kelly muttered and reached for the knob.

"STOP!" cried a man's voice.

Kelly spun around and was prepared to run. Across the kitchen, in the dining room, standing by an open door stood a bearded fireman with no shirt under his heavy jacket. He had an ax swung over one shoulder that he swung down and set on the floor as he crossed toward Kelly.

He thought of running, but realized that he was just as big as this fireman now, in fact as he got closer, Kelly could see that he was taller. For the first time in his life, he stood his ground as a muscular man strode toward him and it felt good!

"The voice warned me that none of us can leave!" the fireman said. "If any of us do, we are all stuck in these bodies for at least a year!" He pushed past Kelly and turned the deadbolt before latching the chain. "I don't know about you, Kelly, but I don't think I can handle a year with a dick!"

"How did you know my name?" Kelly asked. His head was still spinning.

The fireman took a deep breath like he had just been asked the stupidest question. "I'm a fireman." he said as though this explained everything.

"Ok?" Kelly trailed off.

The fireman rolled his eyes. "In the car, I told you I liked firemen! The voice said he was giving us our fantasies and now I'm a fireman! YOU said you liked lifeguards and poof! There you are!"

Kelly shook his head. "Oh my God! Stacy?" He rolled over everything that he had just said and his eyes went wide. "So that means the boys..."

"I expect to find a slutty camp counselor and cheerleader somewhere around this house!" Stacy finished. "Unless one of them was lying," he continued. "There might be another guy for all we know."

"Well it won't be Bruce." Kelly said.

Stacy looked at him under his stern eyebrows.

"He and I have...you know..." Kelly went on.

"Lovely," Stacy said.

"Uh, speaking of." Kelly continued.

Stacy nodded, "The rest of the curse. I heard it too."

"Well," Kelly said, "We need to break it."

"Yeah," Stacy said, looking down at the tent in Kelly's shorts.

"Have you ever blown a guy before?" Kelly asked, stepping up to Stacy and running a finger down his exposed chest. His hand slipped under Stacy's waistband and wrapped around the other man's cock. It was just as hard as Kelly's.

"Oh weird!" Stacy muttered, "My balls move too!"

"I can feel them," Kelly whispered as he opened his hands and gently stroked Stacy's scrotum.

"We uh… should we uh…" Stacy stammered as he walked backwards.

Kelly pulled his hands back out of Stacy's pants and put them on his shoulders, pushing the coat off to fall on the kitchen floor and exposing the red suspenders holding up his pants. "We have to if we want to change back!" Kelly said. "We have to have sex in these bodies!"

Stacy had backed up to a kitchen chair, Kelly looming over him.

"The voice wasn't specific to the details," Stacy said.

"Oral sex is sex!" Kelly said. "I'll blow you, then you can blow me!"

Stacy seemed to finally commit and he pushed forward into Kelly, grabbing him by the shoulders and kissing him hard. As he did so he turned Kelly around so that his back was to the table. "I'll go first!" Stacy said and fell to his knees in front of Kelly. He reached up and pulled Kelly's shorts down. Kelly's cock sprung up to point almost at the ceiling and Stacy looked at it surprised.

"Fantasy cock," Kelly said devilishly.

Stacy looked down for a second and then back up at Kelly, a shy gesture that looked very out of place from a bearded muscular firefighter. "I've done this before but not all the way."

"I think I need to cum for it to work," Kelly said.

Stacy smiled up at Kelly. "This is gonna be weird."

"Just get it over with!" Kelly said.

Stacy opened his mouth and wrapped his lips around the head of Kelly's dick. Kelly shuddered in surprise. He had felt that kind of stimulation on his clit before but never spread over such a large surface. As Stacy began licking, Kelly curled his fingertips under the chair. It was so strange feeling this...outside his body. He could tell that the underside and the ridge were so much more sensitive and he felt himself getting even harder to the point that he felt actual pressure from inside his dick.

"Jesus Christ!" he exclaimed.

Stacy looked up questioningly with Kelly's cock still in his mouth.

"It's so... weird!" he explained. "Good, but... wow! It's weird."

He ran his hands over his own chest and was disappointed at the lack of reaction that elicited. He had no idea men's chests were so unfeeling. He balled his fists wanting a way to push farther toward an orgasm. He began shifting his hips, thrusting his cock into Stacy's mouth, realizing that he had been on the receiving end of boyfriends doing this in the past and had hated it. Now he understood. The male body wanted to thrust. He felt the tension building in his balls and around the base of his dick as Stacy continued to lick and slurp. It was starting to gain pressure. Suddenly, much sooner than Kelly had anticipated he felt a pleasurable throbbing pulse in his cock and felt fluid erupt into Stacy's mouth.

Stacy rocked backward and off his cock immediately and the next pulse shot a white rope across Stacy's red beard.

"No! It has to go in!" Kelly grunted as he pushed Stacy's head back at his crotch. Stacy held back for a second and then reluctantly opened his mouth again to catch the next pulse and the one after that. Kelly gave another grunt and a sigh. He felt the echoes of pleasure around the base of his cock and balls but not much else. He slumped back disappointed. Stacy kept sucking and swallowing the last dribbles. It ceased to be pleasurable as the area grew over-sensitive while he softened.

"Stop." Kelly sighed. "I'm done." It felt like an admission of defeat. He had honestly been looking forward to seeing what it was like as a guy and he felt kind of let down. It was good, and it was different to have it all focused on one organ outside the body, but he missed the tingles and the waves of the female orgasm. It wasn't worse, it just wasn't what he was expecting.

Stacy was trying to wipe the cum out of his beard and only spreading it across more of his whiskers.

"You're going to need water," Kelly explained.

Stacy looked up at him and then stood up to go to the sink. He first washed his mouth out and then ran it over his beard before drying off with a dish towel.

"Sorry about the taste!" Kelly said.

"No," Stacy replied as he finished toweling off. "It was fine, kind of sweet, like uh pineapple."

Kelly grinned. "Of course," he said, shaking his head. "Fantasy cock, fantasy cum."

"So that's not what it usually tastes like," Stacy asked.

Kelly shook his head. "Sorry, sweetie. A guy would have to be a vegetarian on an all melon and pineapple diet for a few days to get this flavor." He stood up and pulled his trunks back up as he spoke. "I knew a guy in high school who talked me into taste testing his experiment."

"Oh!" Stacy replied.

Kelly gave Stacy a guilty look. "Slutty, I know."

"I wasn't going to say anything," he replied.

Kelly shook his head. "It was in your expression." He stepped back from the chair. "Do you want it standing or do you want to sit down?"

Stacy coughed. "I hadn't uh," he looked around, "I don't know, I... He took a step back and leaned against the counter. "Let's try standing," he said.

Kelly licked his lips and crossed the kitchen to him. Gave him a kiss on the lips. Stacy's beard was soaking wet and still dripping. Kelly traced his lips down his chin to his neck, to his chest, down his belly. He slid his fingers under Stacy's suspenders and slid them off his shoulders and then pulled his pants to the ground.

Stacy was not wearing any underwear and his cock sprang up to meet Kelly's lips. With his lips wrapped around the man's cock, Kelly knelt down and wrapped both hands around it, shocked at its size. Clearly Stacy had a dirtier mind than they had given the little princess. Rather than take its massive length into his throat and risk gagging, Kelly focused on the tip for a few moments.

Stacy adjusted his feet and gasped, letting Kelly know that he was doing something right. He slid his tongue and lips down the man's shaft and then spent time nibbling and licking his balls before coming back up and taking him into his mouth again. Because of his size, Kelly's mouth was getting tired and his jaw was starting to ache when he felt the twitch followed by the hot sticky fluid that filled his mouth. It tasted just like Kelly remembered from that high school experiment. Salty sweet with a hint of pineapple and strawberry. Whatever this magic was, it must have been adapting as it went.

He swallowed the first mouthful and then finished sucking the last dribbles dry before sitting back and looking up at Stacy who was standing open-mouthed against the counter.

"Wow," the fireman said. "That was intense and so strange!" he said. "Having an extra appendage is freaky enough but when it did that... oh my."

"Yeah," Kelly agreed. They both sat in stunned silence in the silent kitchen.

Finally, Stacy spoke up, "We gotta go find the guys, let them know what they need to do."

At that moment, they heard a girly squeal of pleasure from down the hall.

"I think they figured it out," Kelly said, climbing to his feet as Stacy pulled up his pants and pulled his suspenders back up. "Come on!"

4, Bruce

Bruce looped her manicured fingers through the straps of Marcus' harness and pulled her up on top. Marcus' face glistened with moisture as the two girls kissed. Bruce rolled them over so that she was on top and then began working her way down to Marcus' chest. Even laying on her back, the corset kept her tits pressed together with dramatic cleavage between them. Bruce ran her nose and lips down to the frilly top and tried to pull it down to expose her breast but the corset boning was firm. She looked at the metal swing hooks holding it closed and grinned as she lifted the top hook out of its loop and the corset began to open, pushed apart by Marcus' breasts. Click, she flipped the next one and could see her bare skin between the sides. Click, the next hook swung up, and the next. The corset flew open to lay on either side of Marcus exposing her dramatically large and round breasts. The areolas were as big around as Bruce could open her mouth as she suckled Marcus' nipple.

Marcus whispered, "Oh god, what the fuck?" as Bruce suddenly felt fluid fill her mouth. It tasted like almond milk with sugar. She lifted her head and looked up at Marcus who had a mortified expression on her face.

“Did I just milk you?” Bruce asked.

“Fuuuuuck!” Marcus said, laying her head back. “I always thought it was hot!”

“It kinda is,” Bruce admitted and then went back to sucking, enjoying the taste of the warm milk as it filled her mouth.

“Ooooh, God! It feels so weird!” Marcus said. “Please stop!”

Bruce picked up her head and wiped her mouth with the back of her hand. “Fine, I’ll just suck your clit instead.” She crawled backward, tracing her hand down from Marcus’ breast to her belly button, over her skirt, and then up under her shiny silk panties. She started to pull them down and they hit the garter straps that hooked to her fishnets. “Oh dammit!” she said as she began fiddling with the clasps. In the dim light, she couldn't see what she was doing. Finally, in a fit of frustration, she yanked on the strap and it slipped out of her hand, snapping back and slapping Marcus’ thigh.

“Ow! Dammit!” Marcus exclaimed in her breathy voice.

“That’s why you put your underwear OVER your stockings and garters.” said a man’s voice from the library door.

Bruce shrieked and fell back onto her ass as she scooted against the wall. Marcus rolled over and got up on her knees, the weight of her now unbound breasts making her topple forward for a moment until she caught the floor with one hand while throwing her other hand over her tits in a vain attempt at covering herself.

Two men stood at the door. Both were tall, broad-shouldered, and muscular. One glistened in the low light of the room, his chest and face hairless, his features chiseled and his eyes blue. He wore only a pair of red shorts that said "Guard" on the leg. The other had red hair combed straight back and a full red beard. He wore red suspenders over a bare, hairy chest that held up a baggy pair of fireman's pants.

Marcus, on her knees, scooted back against the wall too. "Oh shit!" she exclaimed.

The two girls looked up at the strange men in a new terror they had never felt before, knowing that they were exposed, alone, and could be overpowered with no effort.

"Relax guys." said the fireman as he stepped into the room. "It's just us." he pointed at himself, "Stacy," he then pointed at the lifeguard, "and Kelly."

"Oh my God!" Bruce said as she climbed to her feet trying to regain some dignity. "You startled me!" Though standing she still had to look up at the two men. "So you got transformed too?"

Stacy nodded. "Yeah, us too."

Marcus crawled forward quickly and grabbed her corset, holding it backward over her breasts. "Uh, how long were you there?"

"Long enough milky," Kelly said.

Marcus looked down at her tits "oh, shit!"

"We were uh," Bruce tried to explain. "We uh, need to," she began again.

"To break the spell," Marcus added.

"We needed to," Bruce went on.

"To fuck," Kelly finished for them, "Stacy figured it out." he pointed at the fireman. "We blew each other in the kitchen already."

Bruce opened her mouth to say something and then changed her mind.

"Kelly!" Stacy exclaimed in a very un-firemanly way.

"Oh," Marcus said.

"So you two better finish up so we can get back to normal." Kelly went on and then sat in one of the chairs near the door.

Bruce and Marcus just balked. "Are you going to watch?" Marcus asked.

"Nothing better to do." Kelly shrugged and looked up to Stacy who looked back and forth between them before taking a seat in the other chair.

Bruce turned to Marcus and got down on her knees, getting back to the fasteners. After fiddling for a second she looked over her shoulder at the guys. "Can one of you help me?"

Kelly stood up and walked across the room. He towered over Marcus, whose eyes were level with Kelly's shoulders. Kelly went down on one knee and put his hand on Marcus' thigh.

Marcus shivered at his touch. Standing there, in a miniskirt, panties and stockings with her tits hanging out and a man's hand on her thigh, she was extremely and uncomfortably aware of how girly she was. As she felt Kelly's strong fingers manipulate the fasteners and then the loosening on her waist and thighs as they came free, she desperately wanted to be a man again.

"Getting warmer!" the disembodied voice sang.

Everyone looked around in dismay.

The garters loose, Kelly stood up and backed away while Bruce pulled Marcus down to the floor.

"Cold!" the voice said.

Kelly sat down.

"Freezing!" it sang.

Marcus closed her eyes, "Come on!" she said.

Bruce pulled Marcus' panties down and off her legs, pushed her legs apart and came up between them. She licked her lips and parted Marcus' labia with her fingers before lowering her face down and licking her clit.

"ICE COLD!" exclaimed the voice.

"Finger me!" Marcus gasped.

Kelly and Stacy both shifted in their seats.

Bruce pushed his middle finger up inside Marcus who gasped. Bruce added his ring finger while Marcus moaned and, while stroking Marcus' inside with them, she went back to licking her now soaking clit.

"Right action, wrong organ!" said the voice.

"Oh shit!" said Stacy who had just sat up straight in his chair.

"What?" Kelly asked.

Stacy shook her head. “Act out our fantasies!” she said. She looked horrified at Kelly, “In your fantasies, was your dream guy ever blowing another guy?”

Kelly went pale. “You mean…”

Bruce lifted his face out of Marcus’ crotch and looked over her tits at the two guys. “No!”

Stacy sighed. “We have to fuck them.”

“BINGO!” said the voice.

5, Marcus

The four were each seated in a wingback chair in the library. Marcus was holding the open corset over her chest, unable to figure out how to close it and unwilling to ask for help in the awkward silence they all faced. She felt a dribble of milk trail down her breast and run down her belly. Her crotch was wet and she wished she had picked her panties up off the floor before she had sat down. She looked at them now, shiny, black, and damp, laying in the middle of the floor between all four of them like a symbol of her embarrassment.

Bruce had thought to snag hers and had pulled them on before she sat. Across the room, on either side of the door, Kelly and Stacy each tried very hard not to make eye contact or have their eyes linger too long on the panties on the floor, or the exposed pussy between Marucs' legs. Too late she thought to cross them.

She heard a clock start to chime the hour. One, Two, Three, Four. How did so much of the night pass already? It was only about midnight when they had rolled up in the truck. She remembered what the voice had said. They had only tonight to break the spell or they would have to live in those bodies for a whole year. Would she be lactating the whole year? She didn't know how that worked. Where would she get clothes? She thought about Kelly and Stacy and looked down. Her tits would be far too big for anything they had. "Stupid male fantasy," she muttered to herself.

"What?" Stacy asked. His deep voice cutting through the silence.

"I just don't think I can handle these tits for a whole year!" Marcus said.

"Well, I'm not crazy about being stuck with a dick for a year either," Kelly gestured at his lap. His trunks were visibly tented again. "How the fuck do you manage this thing?"

"You get used to it." Marcus said.

Kelly gritted his teeth, "I don't WANT to get used to it, I want to get rid of it!"

"Well, the same goes for these funbags!" Marcus snapped back.

"That is a disgusting word!" Stacy interrupted.

Marcus stood up dropping the corset so that her massive tits hung free, "The're on me! I get to call them whatever I want! Funbags, melons, hooters, tits, bazongas, boobs.."

"You think it's bad now, wait till you get your period!" Stacy mocked.

"STOP IT!" screeched Bruce, her shrill voice cutting over everyone else. "Lets just fucking do it and get it over with!"

The room got silent again as they all looked at her and then at each other.

"Look, we all know each other's fantasies so we all know that none of us is gay," Bruce went on in a measured tone. "If you were trying to prove that you were less gay than the next person," she took a deep breath, "NOW IS NOT THE TIME!" she shouted. "So, Marcus, nut up and get fucked."

Marcus' jaw hung open while Bruce turned to the two men. "Kelly, Stacy, pick one and fuck us so we can get the fuck out of here."

She began unbuttoning her blouse. "But we will NEVER talk about this to anyone ever again!" she said.

Kelly and Stacy looked at each other and then at the girls. Marcus stood in shock, still topless.

Bruce's blouse was now open exposing her white underwire bra. She sighed loudly, grabbed Stacy by the hand, and pulled him out of the room. "I'm betting there are fully furnished bedrooms upstairs." She led Stacy into the central hall and up the wooden stairs.

Marcus looked at Kelly and shrugged. She motioned toward the door and the Lifeguard followed Bruce and Stacy. Marcus took a moment to pick up her corset and panties then followed him up.

Bruce and Stacy disappeared into the first door on the right and closed the door. Kelly stopped at the second door and waited for Marcus. "Bruce was right," he said and waited for Marcus to look in.

There was a large four poster bed sitting in the middle of the far wall with a cloth decorated canopy and rich linens. Marcus' stomach dropped as she walked tentatively into the room, her eyes locked on the bed. Her heart nearly lept out of her throat when the door closed behind her. Kelly walked past her to the bed and sat down, patting a spot next to him.

"I was scared my first time too," he said.

"I've had sex before!" Marcus protested.

Kelly smiled, "You've fucked girls before. You have never been fucked as a girl before. It's different."

"You've never fucked a girl as a guy before." Marcus said.

"Yeah, but I know how vulnerable you feel right now, and..." she shrugged. "Was your fantasy girl a virgin?"

"No." Marcus said. "No, I imagined her, er me, uh....her to be kinda slutty."

Kelly nodded. "Well, at least it won't hurt then. It always hurts the first time for girls."

Marcus sat on the bed, setting her corset and panties at the foot. She felt Kelly's hand on her thigh. "You don't seem nervous." she said.

"I have a different problem." Kelly said and looked down. His trunks were stretched upward into a tent. "I didn't think I was gay." he said. "But the thought of fucking you still has me hard as a rock!"

"Maybe it's the spell." Marcus said. "You wanted a guy who was always ready."

"You think?" Kelly asked.

Marcus looked down at the bulge, it was huge, larger than her cock had been by far. She was terrified about what it would feel like being pushed into her but at the same time, she felt a tingle in her groin and, as she shifted her legs, a wetness in her pussy. "Yeah." she said. "You said you just got a blowjob, but you were already hard when you met us in the library."

"So?" Kelly asked.

"Guys don't work like that." Marcus said. "We nut, then we have to rest for a while before we get hard again."

"Oh." said Kelly.

"Plus." Marcus added. "I'm not into guys, but I'm dripping down there right now."

Kelly laughed.

Marcus looked behind her and then laid flat on the bed. "I guess missionary is the best option." She said. She swallowed hard. Her heart was racing. She felt her boobs pull down on either side of her chest. Kelly stood up and pulled his swim trunks down. His cock was massive, both long and wide with a large flared head. "Oh Jesus," she said as her stomach churned in anticipation.

Kelly looked down at Marcus on her back and paused. "Shit, I can't believe I'm going to fuck a girl." He took a deep breath as he turned and crawled up on the bed between Marcus's open legs. His cock was hovering right over Marcus' pussy. Kelly took a deep breath. "I always wondered what this felt like," he admitted.

"Me too," Marcus confessed. "The four of us may be the only ones to ever know."

"Are you ready?" Kelly asked.

Marcus scrunched up her face and bit her black lipstick-clad lip. "No." She looked Kelly in the eyes. "But do it anyway!"

Kelly breathed deep and thrust. His cock pressed into Marcus' clit for a second and slid up over Marcus' belly.

"You missed!" Marcus said.

"I know!" Kelly replied. "I don't exactly know how to aim this thing!"

Marcus reached down and, for the first time in his life, grabbed another man's cock. She suppressed a shiver and then found the tip with her thumb. She guided it to her pussy and pushed the head in. Once between her lips, Kelly pushed the rest of the way and Marcus gasped in shock, pleasure, and confusion at the sensation of the massive member penetrating deep into her body.

"Oh my God, I'm in!" Kelly exclaimed. "You still ok!"

Marcus nodded and let out a squeak. The pressure inside her was something she could never have imagined before. As Kelly started to pump his hips the waves of sensation from deep inside her pelvis were unprecedented in her entire life. She knew she was having sex with a man and the idea was foreign and unwanted, but no longer disgusting. At the same time, her body was radiating in pleasurable sensation from inside her belly out to every tip of every toe. She felt it building as he kept thrusting and Marcus suddenly and surprisingly overwhelmed as a massive burst of ecstasy washed over her and she cried out in a cross between a cry and a song.

Kelly kept pumping away and Marcus' first climax was almost immediately followed by a building to a second. Her hips radiated sensation from the joints, she had pins and needles down her thighs it was like Kelly's cock was electrical, sending surges of pleasure through her entire body, unlike anything she had ever felt before. "Oh GOD!" she squeaked out as Kelly stared intently into her eyes.

"Is..it..good?" Kelly asked one word on each thrust.

"Yes!" Marcus whimpered.

"Feels..good..here.. too," Kelly panted thrusting deeper now.

"Oooh," Marcus replied followed by a moaning grunt as the second climax finally crashed. She threw her arms up on either side of her head and gripped the sheets in her fists twisting. Her mouth fell open and she gasped for air. She only was able to take a few more breaths before her third climax washed over the receding waves of the second and she let out the most girlish high pitched shriek either of them had ever heard.

At that moment Kelly trusted even deeper and sputtered out "Oh God!" before grunting.

Marcus felt Kelly's cock spurt warm fluid inside her, filling her, her body delighted in the sensation while her mind reeled in disgust, she was filled with cum. Kelly pushed even deeper and she felt it squish around as more and more was pumped into her. "AAAAAwwwwwwwwwwwwwgggggghh," Kelly moaned. "So much better than before!" He finally purred in his deep manly voice by Marcus' ear. He pulled back and Marcus felt the cum spill out of her and run down her ass.

"Oh God, I'm leaking!" she said as she lifted herself up on her elbows. She felt a trickle from her nipples that told her that her cunt wasn't the only thing leaking at that moment.

Kelly grabbed a corner of the blanket and threw it up over Marcus' crotch. "Yeah, it drips out a bit if it isn't wrapped," he said. He then grabbed the sheet that had been exposed and wiped the moisture off his dick.

From the room next door they heard Bruce's shrill scream in delight. "Sounds like Stacy is getting it done too."

Marcus was wiping the last drops off her pussy and dabbing a corner of the blanket against her tits to soak up the extra milk. "So we should be changing back soon?"

"I hope so," Kelly said. "Though this wasn't so bad, and you sounded like you enjoyed yourself."

Marcus blushed. "I don't know if it was me or this body." She looked down at the tits and dickless crotch below her. "But I think I orgasmed like three times."

"Fantasy cock," Kelly said as he pulled his trunks back on. "It cums quick and tasty from a blowjob, but it fucks hard and long till she cums 3 times." she sighed. "It's what I always dreamed of in a man."

Marcus reached for her panties and pulled them on, lifting her ass for a moment to slide them up.

"Goddammit!" she said and grabbed the blanket to wipe up another drop that had leaked out. "Was it your fantasy for him to dump a gallon in you?!"

"I think they call it a breeding kink," Kelly said sheepishly. "Sorry."

Marcus picked up the corset and wrapped it around her again but she couldn't get the clasps together.

"You need to loosen the laces," Kelly explained and came over, taking the corset out of Marcus' hands and laying it flat on the bed so he could untie and begin pulling the laces loose. "Wrap it, close it, then pull it tight," he explained.

The noises from the next room died down.

"Well done! Well played!" the cheery voice announced. "You had your treat within my trick! I don't suppose you want this to stick?"

"Give us our bodies back!" Marcus called out at the ceiling.

"You speak for one, but not for all!" the voice sang. "Do all four of you repeat this call?"

"YES!" yelled Kelly.

They heard Bruce's high pitch "Yes" from next door.

There was a pause. Marcus and Kelly looked at each other in dismay. Finally, Stacy's baritone voice said, "Yes Spirit! Change us back!" but the voice sounded unsure.

Marcus raised an eyebrow and Kelly shrugged.
"I suspect one of you would like this to stick, do not lose hope as I have a final trick!" the voice announced.
Marcus fell back on the bed feeling defeated as her massive tits flopped down on her.
The voice went on, dropping out of rhyme again. The trickster seemed to have no consistency in its taunting games.
"I promised your bodies back so that I will grant, but who gets which is still up to you."
"What!?" Bruce's voice cried out in the other room.
The cheery voice went on, but there was an edge to it now. "You came to steal from me, a stone gargoyle from my roof!"
"We can leave it!" Marcus pleaded.
"Leave it and stay as you are, not for a year but forever!" The voice had lost all cheer now. "No, you must play this last game."
"What do we have to do?" asked Kelly.
"Choose," the voice said.
"There are four Gargoyles on my roof! Each decides a different mix," the voice announced. "The partners swap, the partners cross, the boys and girls swap with each other, or they all go back to normal."
"You mean," Marcus asked, "depending on which one we take, I could end up in any of the other bodies?"
"You understand!" the voice had regained its sing-song cheer, "Now play!"

Marcus and Kelly looked at each other.

"Finish getting that thing on me," Marcus said at last. "We have a choice to make."

Kelly got back to pulling laces, his hand shaking. "How are we going to choose?"

6, Stacy

The four gargoyles looked different than they had when they pulled up. Though they retained their leathery wings and clawed feet the grotesque faces and bodies had taken on a more human shape. Stacy could swear that one looked just like the general whose statue they intended to replace, another looked like goth Marcus with oversized bosoms covered by clawed hands, and the third like lifeguard Kelly tall and muscular. Stacy didn't recognize the fourth.

“It looks just like Mr. Landon.” Bruce said “This was his property before he gifted it to the camp.”

Stacy knew then what to do. The easy choice for their prank was the general. But whatever spirit had been toying with them didn’t seem like one to give an easy answer. “The original owner for our original bodies!” she declared.

The others looked at each other nervously. They each nodded.

Kelly and Stacy lifted the statue from its stand.

7, Finale

In the central square on campus on the morning of November 1st a crowd had gathered around the fountain. Where the old General, founder of the College had once stood, a grotesque stone gargoyle, its original shape restored as soon as it had left the property, had taken its place, standing amid a mountain of red bubbles. Off to the side, leaning against Marcus' truck, the four friends admired their work.

"Looks amazing," Stacy said as she rested her head on Bruce's shoulder.

Bruce just nodded in agreement.

Kelly looked down at her watch, "Shit! I have swim practice in fifteen minutes. UGH!" she sighed. "I am going to drag all day!"

Marcus put his hand on Kelly's shoulder. "Could be worse."

"I could be you!" Kelly smirked.

"Yeah, lucky for us that we made the right choice," Marcus admitted.

Kelly leaned in. "Wouldn't be all bad." She kissed Marcus on the lips. "I could stand to fuck your tight pussy with my throbbing cock again."

Marcus's eyes went wide with shock. He looked

past Kelly at Stacy and Bruce who seemed just as surprised as Marcus was.

Kelly looked at him under her eyebrows. "I can't wait to see if you can give as good as you got." She winked and walked off toward the campus aquatic facility.

Marcus remained frozen in place with his jaw agape. He was finally snapped out of his stupor when Bruce punched him on the shoulder.

"So, Stacy and I were talking," Bruce said. "Wanna go back to the house next Halloween?"

Marcus just blinked for a moment. A grin slowly crossed his face. "Yeah, I think I do."

Broken Trust

Mike pulled into his parking space outside the townhouse and just slumped in his seat for a while. When he got the call to come in on his day off, he knew that something was wrong. His eyes drifted to the folder in the passenger seat. "Severance Agreement" was printed in plain letters on the front. One month of pay and then he was shit out of luck.

He looked up, Ben's car was where he had left it, still as pristine as it had been a month ago when he had it custom delivered. His roommate was lucky enough to work from home and make twice what Mike made. Maybe he could get Mike a job if only Mike understood what the hell it was that Ben did.

He let out one final puff, grabbed his severance packet, and made his way into their townhouse. The ground floor was empty. He could hear Ben on a conference call upstairs. On the counter was a stack of mail including a large padded manilla envelope addressed to Ben.

Sorting through the rest, Mike found two envelopes addressed to him. Both were bills he wouldn't be able to pay unless he could find work fast. He tossed the bills back on the stack and upended the fridge.

Luckily, Ben bought good beer and had repeatedly given Mike an open invitation to drink what he liked. He snagged a bottle with a German name and almost tore his hand before he realized it needed a bottle opener. He set the bottle cap against the countertop and smacked it down with his hand.

The counter chipped and a chunk split away while the cap remained in place, except for one small piece that had bent enough to allow a spray of foam to shoot all over the kitchen.

"SHIT" Mike shouted as he stuck the spraying bottle in his mouth and dropped his severance packet into the puddle of beer on the floor.

Mike quickly looked around for the bottle opener, popped the top, and set the foaming beer in the sink before he saw his severance packet soaking up fluid on the floor.

"GodDamnit!" He bellowed as he bent down and lifted it. Beer dripped from the back pages. He pulled out several sheets of paper towels and laid them on the counter, and then dropped the Severance packet on top of it. He then picked up the beer bottle, surveyed the mess in the kitchen, and said "Fuck it!" before walking out to the living room and collapsing on the couch. He picked up the remote but the TV wouldn't respond to any button press.

"Not dealing with it!" he said to himself and just sat in the dark where he nursed his beer in silent aggravation.

He was swishing the dregs in the beer bottle when he heard Ben come down the stairs cheerfully. 0

"Hey, dude! I heard you come in and...HOLY FUCK! What happened to the Kitchen?" Ben said in surprise.

"Grab me another Beer!" Mike called from the

couch.

He heard Ben pulling out paper towels

"I'll get it in a minute! That's my mess!" Mike called.

"I got ya, bud!" his roommate replied.

After a few minutes, Mike heard the 'pop' of a bottle open, and Mike walked in holding two beers by the neck in one hand and a leather-bound book in the other. He set a beer on the table in front of Mike.

"Drink up! I saw the folder." Ben said sympathetically.

"Yeah," Mike said. He finished the last drops from the bottle in his hand before swapping for the new cold bottle Ben had just brought in. "Fun day for me!" He took a long drink.

"Well, don't worry too much, I can cover expenses for a bit if need be." Ben replied.

Mike closed his eyes. "Buddy, don't take this the wrong way, but..."

"But you don't want your best friend paying your way. Fine, I'll charge you interest!" Ben said and offered a toast.

Mike looked at the raised bottle for a long time before he clinked it with his "Only if I need it." He said. "I'm Job hunting full-time as of tomorrow morning!"

"You'll find something," Ben said with a sly grin and picked up the TV remote.

"Oh, That..." Mike began but the TV turned on as soon as Ben pressed a button. "Never mind, I must have had it at a bad angle."

Ben put on a SciFi show they had both rewatched a half dozen times, mainly as background noise.

Mike started scrolling through his phone. His coworkers who had also been laid off were having a "pink slip" party at one of their apartments. Mike contemplated going and looked over to Ben to see if he wanted to come. Ben was flipping through the old leather bound journal.

"What is that?" Mike asked.

Ben didn't look up. "I'm not sure." He flipped a page. "My folks always said my Uncle Otis had joined some sort of cult out west, so I only saw him a couple of times when I was little. Well apparently, he died last week and this was sent to me from his effects." He held the book up and showed it to MIke.

"Is it his diary?" Mike asked.

Ben shook his head. "The guy was a wacko. This is some sort of cross between a manifesto, a diary, a compendium of grievances and a spell book."

"Spellbook?" Mike repeated.

"Well no, maybe. Look, here he talks about a ritual to curse your enemies. Then, for like the next 5 pages he goes on a tirade listing people who had wronged him and how he cursed them." He flipped a few pages and held it up for Mike "Look! My Mom is right there. Apparently, she ensnared my dad with her witchcraft!"

Mike nodded. "Nuts"

"Not just nuts, but a sexist asshole too!" Ben went

on. "He keeps coming back to his attempts to conjure the perfect female, both submissive and devoted to him."

"Conjure?" Mike asked.

"Well, that's the thing." Ben said "He claimed that, since the perfect girl couldn't exist in an imperfect world, he had no choice but to create one from what he could find"

Mike raised his eyebrows. "Wow, not subtle at all"

"Nope," Ben agreed.

"Maybe that was his wank-bank." Mike offered.

Ben closed the book and looked at him. "What!?"

"What if it was no more than your uncle's fantasy? Conjuring a perfect woman out of an imperfect one. Maybe he got off on the idea and liked to pretend." Mike explained

Ben blinked for a moment, "Yeah.. Ewww. But yeah that would make sense, except..."

"Except?" Mike asked.

"Except the date Otis wrote next to my Mom's name when he cursed her was my 10th birthday. The day she broke her leg falling down the stairs getting a camera to take my picture." Ben said.

Mike set his beer down, now invested. "So, you're saying, your crazy uncle Otis, from across the continent, was able to cast a MAGIC spell that made your Mom fall down the stairs when she happened to be rushing around at her kid's birthday?"

"When you say it that way," Ben admitted. He closed the book and set it on the table and the two of them watched the end of the episode.

The next show was not one they cared for too much, but there was nothing else to do so they just slumped into their two couches and sipped beer.

Mike noticed Ben's hand wandering to the book and brushed it a few times before moving to the beer bottle.

"So." Mike broke the silence. "What would she be like?"

Ben feigned confusion "Sorry?"

"Your perfect woman. I know you're thinking about it." Mike said. "And don't give me the bullshit answer you would tell some girl! Get dirty with it!"

Ben shook his head and didn't answer. He looked at the two empty bottles and went to the kitchen.

"Big Tits obviously!" He called from the refrigerator.

"Obviously!" Mike agreed.

"Brown hair, Long," Ben said as he brought back two more bottles.

"Not blond?" Mike asked.

"Nah.. Blonds are... just too ..... Nah.." Ben said

"Eloquent" Mike nodded.

"Curvy but not fat. In fact, she would be incapable of getting fat no matter how much she ate." Ben said.

"Something, for her." Mike smiled.

"She wouldn't wear much, and what she did wear was always sexy, like guys cum in their pants when she walks past, but she would only ever consider being with me," Ben said.

"Now you're getting into it." Mike nodded, "What about her personality?"

Ben sat and thought for a moment. "She would have to be herself. Most of the time at least. I mean, in the end, she would do what I said but outside outright commands, I wouldn't want her to be like a robot or anything."

"Ok," Mike said sitting up. "Bullshit!"

"Pardon?" Ben asked

"She can't be herself and also be your obedient servant. If she was herself then she wouldn't obey when given a command she didn't want to follow. If she was compelled to obey then she would do it robotically and then spend the rest of her time hating you for doing that to her." Mike said. "Paradox"

"Well what if she WANTED to obey?" Ben asked.

Mike shook his head. "That fucks with free will, she wouldn't be herself."

Ben was silent for a moment. "She is addicted to my cum! Like she goes into withdrawal if she doesn't get it every day."

"That just makes her a junkie," Mike said. "I hated cigarettes long before I could quit them."

"Point," Ben said as he picked up the book again and leafed through it. "Wonder if Otis thought this out?"

Mike shrugged and went back to watching TV.

"Perception!" Ben blurted out.

Mike hit mute on the TV. "What are you talking

about?"
"The dream girl," Ben said. "Otis fixed the free will paradox with perception."
Mike thought about it. "Wait, you said fixed? As in he did it?"
Ben was looking at the journal. "According to this, his dream woman was never able to see a reason not to obey his commands. This was due to a glamor he had cast over the rest of the spell to block her ability to perceive that she was being controlled!"
"He made a dumb bimbo," Mike said.
"Claims she was unchanged from her original personality," Ben said triumphantly. He closed the book. "A perfect girl, under his command, personality intact!"
"Yeah!" Mike scoffed. "I'd like to see it happen!"
"I'm ordering Pizza and putting the Season 3 DVDs on," Ben said.
Mike held up his beer. "I'll drink that!"
It was well after midnight when Mike called it quits and staggered to the stairs. Ben was glassy-eyed watching TV with the journal open on his lap. The table had been covered with empty beer bottles and a pair of empty pizza boxes were on the floor. The place was a mess, but Mike could take a break from job hunting to clear it up.
At the top of the stairs, he shoved the door to his room shut and collapsed on his bed relieved to be at the end of such a bad day.
Thirsty.

The early morning light was poking through the blinds as his mind coalesced around two overwhelming sensations.

He was thirsty, and he had to pee.

Pulling himself out of bed he chastised himself for not taking the proper hangover prevention steps of drinking a shit-ton of water before bed.

He stood up, his balance was wrong and his pants fell to the floor tripping him. He fell forward. He was slow to get his hands up and would have fallen on his face but his chest caught him, painfully. A cascade of brown hair fell around his face as he hit the ground and he let out a surprisingly high-pitched "ooof!"

Surprised by the pain, he rolled over and threw his right hand over his...breasts?

"What the..." he said and noticed the raspy voice was not as deep as it should be. He clenched his hand on the breast it cupped and felt it through his shirt. It was real and it was his. "Oh GOD!" he reached to the neck of his shirt and lifted it to look down at the two mounds of flesh now on his chest.

Mike sat up in shock, feeling the weight shift as he did so. He still had to pee and was terrified at what he would find in the bathroom. His jeans were around his hairless thin ankles, he kicked them off realizing how small his feet seemed and rolled to his feet, hair fell in his field of view as he darted a hand down to catch the waistband of his boxers just before they fell, "Can't look yet!" he said to himself and stumbled against the door frame, pulled the door open and crossed the hall into the bathroom watching the long-haired beauty in the mirror burst in. He paused for a single glance at her before he turned to the toilet and pulled his boxers down.

"Of course." the woman's voice said as Mike looked down at the flat crotch and patch of neatly trimmed hair that framed a pretty slit. Mike was all girl.

The urge to pee was undeniable and she wasn't sure she knew how long she could hold it. Closing her eyes and feeling a tear trickle down her cheek, she sat down and let go hearing a hiss and tinkle while feeling the warm flow from what seemed like a spot under where her dick used to be. "Oh God, Oh God, Oh God!" She kept repeating as the stream seemed endless. When it finished she could feel a few drops clinging to her. She pulled off a few squares from the toilet paper roll, wiped, and flushed before facing the mirror to wash her hands.

She deliberately avoided looking in the mirror but looking down was just as disorienting. Her v-neck t-shirt hung out giving her a look at her a glimpse of her own cleavage as her arms pushed her tits together reaching for the sink.

"These things are fucking huge!" she said as she pressed her elbows into them. She shook her head, no time to play with herself. She focused on her hands, they were slender and dainty with long manicured nails painted a deep reflective red. The

soap bar from the dish felt huge in them.
As she rinsed, the running water reminded her how thirsty she was. She filled the cup she kept beside the sink to brush her teeth and gulped it down. Then a second. It wasn't doing it. She looked at the beautiful woman in the mirror. Her features were stunning! High cheekbones, round face, bow-shaped lips. She licked her lips "God, I'd fuck my brains out." She moaned before downing a third cup of water.
"Ugh! So Thirsty!" She said and pulled open the door.
"Uh Hello!" Ben said. He was standing in the hallway with no shirt on, just his boxers.
Mike looked her roommate over, defined pecs, decent abs, and manly chest hair. She felt moisture between her legs and slapped them together while emitting a muted "umf"
"You..." Ben stammered. "You can't be here!"
"I live here!" Mike pleaded. How was he going to explain to Ben that his best friend and roommate suddenly became a woman?
"No! That was crazy talk!" Ben said. "Uncle Otis was a crackpot! You can't BE HERE!"
Now Mike was even more confused. "Out of my way!" She pushed past Ben into her room and slammed the door.
"But... it shouldn't work!" Ben called. She heard him rushing downstairs.
"Fuck, he's calling the cops," She thought. Looking down she realized she was dressed all wrong if

people were coming over. She pulled open her top drawer and was hit with another shock.

Her clothes, her boy's clothes, were gone. The top drawer was divided, on the right were stacks of women's panties. Not a single pair of cotton granny panties either. Every single pair was frilly, or shiny or lacy, or tiny. On the left side of the drawer was an assortment of stockings and hoses. She was still holding up her boxers from falling so she had little choice. She dropped the boxers to the floor and grabbed a pair of panties. They were black with a lace embroidered front panel and a thong back. She pulled them on, feeling it slide between her buttcheeks and cup her new mound. Almost on autopilot she snatched a pair of black stockings and sat on her desk chair while she watched in amazement as her fingers rolled them up her legs with practiced skill. With her legs encased in nylon and her sex in silk, she opened the next drawer to find that her undershirts had been replaced with bras. Her hand went to a black one with lace cups that perfectly matched the panel on the front of her panties. Her hands, arms, and shoulders knew how to slide it on, dip down to cup her breasts, and then fasten it behind her back without hassle.

“What the...” she said to herself. A couple of weeks earlier, she had completely fumbled trying to unlatch Stacy Saunders's bra at the end of their date. How was she suddenly so good at this? She paused for a moment in shock, looked down, and said aloud, "And why did I put on stockings?" She remembered Ben downstairs. And opened her next drawer. A Black ribbed crop top that she suspected used to be a concert T-shirt was her first choice. She pulled it over her head and over her tits before moving to her closet.

There was not a single pair of pants. Her jeans and work khakis were now a variety of skirts, some straight, some pleated, some contoured, ranging from denim to cotton to leather. On the right side of the closet hung dresses. More dresses than the suits they had replaced. Little black dresses, body-hugging club dresses, Mini-skirted ball gowns. Despite the variety, they all had two things in common, they were low cut and had short skirts, with the exception of one elegant gown that had a slit that seemed to rise up above the waist.

"Ok, weirder and weirder," she said.

Her throat was so dry though she needed to get downstairs and drink something besides water. She grabbed a Denim skirt from the hanger, and pulled it on, zipping it up as she moved toward the door. She halted and looked down at her black-nylon-encased feet, went back to the closet, slipped her feet into a pair of pumps, and then strode confidently out of her bedroom door. Three steps down the hall she suddenly realized that she had put on the shoes, that they had raised heels, and that she was oddly fine walking in them despite toppling over from the weight of her tits only a few minutes earlier. It was like she felt natural walking in heels.

At the bottom of the stairs, she went straight to the refrigerator in the kitchen. There was a red sports drink sitting unopened in the door. She grabbed it, twisted the top off with difficulty and then started gulping it down. The brain freeze hit her and forced her to stop. She doubled over from the pain.

“You can’t be here!” Ben said through the portal between the living room and the kitchen.

“Ben! I live here!” She grunted through the pain and looked up at him.

He had the journal open on the breakfast counter and was looking from it to her and back down. He turned a page, turned back and then looked at Mike once more. “No.” He said. He turned several pages and read.

The pain passed and MIke swallowed another gulp of the sports drink but she was even more thirsty now than when she had woken up. “FUCK! I’m Thirsty!” She said and took another futile gulp. The weird thing was that her stomach felt full despite her thirst. She let out a loud but still, frustratingly girly burp.

“How are you here?” Ben asked again. “Even if it works I don't have a subject!”

“Ben, this is going to sound crazy,” Mike said. “But you are already sounding a little crazy.” She moved over to the counter opposite her roommate. “I’m Mike”

Ben stared at her slack-jawed. He looked down at the book and back at her. “Oh no!” He looked back at the book. "I fucked up!"

"You fucked up?" Mike asked, confused. "I'm standing here in a skirt and you think you..." Suddenly, she stopped and looked at the journal, remembering their conversation from the night before. "Ohhh FUCK!"

"I, I didn't know!" Ben said. "It was gibberish nonsense."

"What, Ben?" Mike asked, "What was gibberish nonsense?"

"This passage at the end." He turned to the back of the book, where several pages held strange symbols with phonetic pronunciations under them. "I didn't like chant them or do any spell stuff, I just read them out loud."

Mike took a deep breath to calm herself but it caused her tits to push out reminding her that she had them which only made her more upset. "You read a mysterious language out loud from a magic book and now I have tits!?" She was almost screeching by the end of the sentence.

"Calm down!" Ben commanded. "I'm sure there is a way to uh... fix this."

Mike realized that getting hysterical wouldn't help the situation and got a hold of herself. She took a deep measured breath. "Ok, so what does the journal say?" she asked.

Ben was scanning and turning pages. "I haven't read the whole thing yet," he said. "But I recognized you as soon as I saw you upstairs."

"I don't look anything like I looked yesterday." she calmly stated.

He shook his head. "No I mean, I recognized the dream girl we thought up last night. Brown hair, big tits, nice curves...."

Mike looked down at herself. "Always dressed sexy," she added. This explained the stockings and pumps. She took another sip of the sports drink even though she was full, her thirst was driving her crazy. She stopped and turned pale. "Uhh, Ben?" she said. "Did it make me, uhhh, exactly as we talked about?" She suddenly had a very bad feeling about her thirst and as soon as she connected the dots in her mind the craving became much more directed and intense. "Oh shit," she said.

Ben looked up. "Well our conversation was kind of my template for a dream girl so I guess it would have done everything we...why are you looking at me like that?"

"The addiction!" Mike whimpered. "I have an addiction to... uhhh" She looked down at Ben's crotch.

"Oh. OhhhhhH!" He stood up from the barstool he was seated on and backed away. "But.. ohhhh crap!"

Mike shook her head. "I know!" She set the bottle down and came around the counter out of the kitchen.

Ben backed away more. "But, you're a guy! You're my best friend."

"It's not like I want to do this!" Mike said and licked her lips. "Well, my body wants it!" She smacked her own head "But in here, yeah, I'm still me! I'm not into guys!" She felt a clenching in her crotch and a renewed wetness in her panties. "But I fucking need it, from you!"

Ben had backed into the wall, Mike was moving up against him. She realized how much shorter she was than him. They used to be about the same height.

"Uhh um...." Ben said. "I'm so sorry!" he said.

Mike's thirst was almost blinding. She looked up into Ben's eyes as she sank to her knees in front of him, her slender fingers passing through the opening in the front of his boxers, wrapping around his hardening cock and pulling it out. "This doesn't seem sorry!" She said in a low accusatory voice.

"You're a hot chick about to blow me, of course, it's hard! Besides, you need it anyway." He replied.

"Need, not want," Mike said. She looked at the penis in her hand and scrunched up her face, a gesture that looked extremely cute and sexy to Ben who only got harder when he saw it. "After this, we are going to find a fix!" She said,

A drop of precum emerged from the tip of Ben's dick. Seeing it, Mike could no longer resist and wrapped her lips around it, sucking greedily.

Ben flattened his hands against the wall on either side of him as his newly feminized best friend hungrily licked and nibbled at his cock.

Mike remembered what he had liked in a blow job and focused on the underside of Ben's cock, flicking her tongue right along the ridge of his head while she gently massaged his balls with her hands. Her thirst was still there, but no longer agonizing, rather she was enjoying the sensation of a cock in her mouth and the thirst kept her at it until she felt Ben's body stiffen. There was a puff in her mouth, followed by a spurt as hot salty cum erupted into her cheeks. She gulped it down greedily and felt immediate satisfaction, even a moment of ecstasy. Once she had sucked every last drop out of him and swallowed it down she rocked her head back and wailed "Fuck this body loves cum!"

"My cum." Ben said.

"Whatever." Mike said as she wiped her mouth across the back of her hand. "It's humiliating as hell though. You need to find a way to fix this before I need another dose! I do NOT want to have to do that again."

"Of course," Ben said. He bent down and pulled up his boxers before returning to the barstool where he had left the book open.

Mike pulled herself to her feet and went back to the kitchen where she found the severance package still on its pile of damp paper towels. She opened it. "Not going to any job interviews like this!" She said, "And none of my IDs either. Thankfully this is direct deposit!"

"Don't worry about money," Ben said without

looking up.

Mike closed the severance folder. "I have bigger problems anyway." She said, "I may as well let you float me seeing as you lost my dick!"

"Good girl," Ben said.

Mike rolled her eyes. "Yeah, that's what I need to hear."

"Nah!" Ben laughed. "You like when I call you a good girl."

Mike smiled at the joke and felt warmth at her friend's attempt to comfort her. "It's not the worst thing," she admitted.

"Go clean up while I read this," Ben said.

Mike looked around the house. It was still a disaster from the night before. She grabbed the green recycling bin and carried it into the living room where she started clearing off the bottles they had left.

By the time she had collected the bottles, trashed the pizza boxes, wiped down the counters, and scrubbed the stove, the garbage was full. She lifted the bag out, marveling at how weak she now was, and was about to take it out to the dumpster

"Wait!" Ben said.

She stopped. Maybe he found a cure.

Ben looked at her thoughtfully. "Missy"

"What?" Mike asked.

"Someone might see you out there. If they ask who you are, your name is Missy" Ben said.

"Ahhh" Missy replied. "Good idea!" She opened the door and strutted out to the bin and back, no one saw her.

When she got back, Ben was no longer looking at the book. “Good girl, Missy,” he said.

She smiled at him. It felt good knowing he was watching out for her. “Find anything in the book?” She asked hopefully.

“Nothing useful,” he said.

Missy crossed to him. “Maybe I should take a look”

Ben put his hand on the book. “You shouldn’t,” he said flatly.

Missy stopped. It was true that Ben had been looking through the book all day yesterday and today. There wasn’t likely anything new that she could find. “Ok,” she said. “But please hurry! I want to change back before I need to do... that ... again” She glanced down at his crotch and was alarmed that she felt a tickle of thirst once more.

“Shhhh,” Ben said as he put his hand on Missy’s shoulder. “You’re not going to worry about the book, or changing back anymore,” He said.

Her face dropped for a moment, something seemed wrong but she didn't know what it was.

Ben smiled and moved his hand down to the bare flesh on the small of her back. “You’re going to let me take care of you as your Master and you’re going to learn to love being my good girl”

Missy’s mind nearly broke for a second and she felt the hot flush of fury but it was immediately washed away by the warm comfort from her Master calling her a good girl.

As he moved his hand down her back to her ass

and pulled her close, he whispered "You know you can feed your addiction with either set of lips. Let's use the lower ones this time" she withheld the impulse to protest as he stood, and led her back up the stairs.

In Ben's room, she laid back on his bed while he pushed her skirt up around her waist and slid her thong aside.

She gasped as her master entered her for the first time. It was pleasurable, painful, and disorienting all at once. Ben's cock was inside her, her brain was having trouble processing the stretching pain between her legs and the sensation of him sliding up and down inside her body. She could feel him impossibly deep in her. As his hips bucked and he thrust repeatedly she fought back her disgust trying to focus on the pleasure her body clearly felt from being fucked. "Oh, God!" she blurted. "I'm being fucked!"

"Yeah baby!" Ben grunted. "Cum for me!"

As he said this, with perfect timing, her eyes rolled back and the waves of pleasure that had been building up in her abdomen seemed to explode and wash over her body. It was like no orgasm she had ever felt as a man. This was deep in her core and seemed to flow out from her pussy to the rest of her body so that even her fingers tingled. She cried out.

"Good..GIRL!" He grunted and began thrusting faster and harder.

Rather than being spent, her body seemed to pick

right up and in moments she was orgasming once more. She whimpered.

“You need me!” He said

She had to admit, he was right. In her mind and in her heart she was still a man named Mike who hated being a girl and hated the idea of being intimate with another man. But her body had an entirely different opinion. Her body was desperate for his cock, and wanted it in her. In her mouth or in her pussy, she just needed it. She knew this was all a result of the addiction they had accidentally given her, but that addiction was real. She was just grateful that Ben was here to help her. She didn’t blame him. They both thought up this dream girl that she now was, and Ben had no way to know that messing with the book would make this happen. Her Master was right, it was best to never touch that book again. She was happy he was there to stop her from making a bigger mistake in the misguided attempt to change back.

The truth was that, as much as she hated the fact that she would be a girl for the rest of her life, she was lucky to have Ben to take care of her. Ben was her best friend, and the only person who could supply the cum that her addiction needed. He had been the one with the wisdom to close the book and leave things as they were, so it made sense that she would call him her Master. As hard as it was going to be to adjust to life as his obedient girlfriend, she owed it to him to try.

She felt Ben thrust deeper than he had before, felt

his cum spurting into her. Her body reacted with warm satisfaction, and she orgasmed for the third time as a woman.

Yes, she owed it to her Master to be a Good girl.

A Mother's Love

Ben clutched his Diploma in his hand, hardly able to believe that he had finished school and earned it. Since his Father had died, his relationship with his mother and his grades had gone to hell, he barely scraped by with a D average, but he had done it. Now it was time to focus on fixing things with Mom. His Mother hadn't even come to see him walk for Graduation. He took a deep breath at the door, hoping that the rift was not already too great to bridge. "Make peace, we need each other, control your temper" He told himself, and then walked inside. "Your Graduate is home!" he announced. He heard the TV in the Kitchen. A news report was talking about the escalating tensions in the Indian Ocean. It quickly turned off and a voice flatly said "In here."

Ben's mother was sitting at the kitchen table. Her black hair with white streaks was pulled back into a tight ponytail. On the table was a closed rectangular case marked "MACR" and Ben's laptop sitting open to the "Password Exchange" site Ben had been using to make side money.

Ben felt the color drain from his face. All thought of reconciliation vanished at that moment. He was in deep trouble.

"How did you find that?!" He asked with a shaky voice.

"Sit Down!" she demanded.

Ben took the seat caddy corner to her. "Mom, it's just for fun I..."

"It's worse than a felony!" She exclaimed "You have passwords to defense industry contractors here. Do you know what that means with everything going on in the world right now? Do you know what that means for me, working for the Defense Department? You'll be considered a traitor. No cops, no trial, you will just disappear, and now that I know about this, I am obligated to report it."

Ben's heart was racing. He felt nauseous. "Please Mom! Don't! I'll wipe the site! No one else knows! Please, I'll do anything!"

Ben's mother put her hand on the rectangular box. "Anything?"

"I have a kill script written, Just let me execute it, it will wipe the site and the drive. Half an hour and all traces of the site will be gone." Ben assured her.

"Fine." She said, "Execute the script, but things are about to change around here, there is an outfit for you in the bathroom."

Ben shot her a curious look as he typed in the command. He paused for a minute to lament the stored data about to be lost and then pressed enter. Then he went into the bathroom. When he saw what was hanging there he exclaimed "FUCK NO!" and stormed back out.

The chair where his mother had been sitting was now empty. The rectangular box was open and showed the empty impression of a syringe in the foam padding. He turned to see where his mother had gone only to find himself face to face with her. He felt a sharp sting in his chest and looked down to see his mother's hand finish pushing the plunger of the syringe all the way down.

Immediately he felt warm and flush. "What? What was that?"

"A new beginning," She said. "Once you are dressed, I will explain what is going on."

"But..." Ben said.

"I made a copy of the data Benjamin. Do as I say or I will have no choice but to make the call" She replied. "No Buts, young lady!"

Ben was stammering "What do you mean young..."

"GO! NOW!" She shouted.

Ben looked down at her for a moment and then walked into the bathroom looking up in disgust at the dress that hung from the shower rod. It had a white blouse with a peter-pan collar and a high waist that flared out into a pleated black skirt. Sitting folded on the toilet seat was a bra, panties, and black tights. A pair of silicone breast forms were laying beside the bra. "Better than prison." He said to himself as he began unbuttoning his shirt.

The panties were smooth but seemed too small, his balls wanted to come out of the sides of the gusset. Ben managed the tights well enough as he had watched his girlfriend Sarah roll pantyhose on after the two of them had lost their virginity to each other on a picnic blanket under the stars after prom only a month ago. The Bra was a front clasp mercifully and seemed to fit the silicone prosthetics perfectly. Once he had pulled on the dress he took a deep breath and stepped out into the now empty kitchen "Upstairs Ben!" His mother called.

At the top of the stairs, Ben found his bedroom door closed but the guest room, which she had kept locked while she worked on remodeling it, was now open for the first time in weeks. Ben went in to find her standing by the closet.

The walls were a bright pink with a vine and rose border. There was a canopy bed in the center of the room covered with a flowery quilt and too many pillows. Against the wall was a long dresser. A makeup table with an oval mirror was against the wall beside the door. "Can you please tell me what you injected me with?" Ben asked as he entered, feeling his skirt brushing against the door frame.

"What do you think of the room?" His mom asked.

"Looks nice." Ben said. "A little girly, but it's pretty."

"Good. Because it's your room now." She said,

"What? Mom! What is going on? Why am I in a dress? What was that stuff?" Ben demanded.

"Remember that case I told you about?" Ben's mother asked"The one with the crazy Doctor who was kidnapping men and turning them completely into women from the inside out using some super-science formula?"

Ben could feel the blood draining from his face. "No! You didn't!" He said breathlessly.

"Modified Accelerated Regrowth Formula." His mom said. "It's top secret, it's experimental, it's irreversible, and over the next two weeks, it will reshape your entire body according to its programmed design."

Ben's world had just exploded. He looked at the room, and then down at the dress he was wearing. His hands drifted up to clutch the fake breasts in his bra. "No!" he gasped.

"Those are C-cups," His mother explained. "MACR isn't exact, but your real ones will be about that size or larger."

"Mom! I don't want to be a girl! Please don't do this!" Ben pleaded. He could feel his pulse thumping through his head. He was dizzy.

"It's already done dear. The nanites are self-replicating, I couldn't stop it now if I wanted to." she said.

"Why?" Ben asked.

"You barely made it out of highschool and you have no prospects for the future. You run around with that slut Sarah, and those losers from your game club. If your father was alive, he would be ashamed." She stepped closer and took Ben by the shoulders. "You failed as a man. So, we are starting over, Mother and Daughter."

"I hate you!" Ben said. He could feel tears rolling down his face.

His mother hugged him close. "I know." She stepped back. "For a while at least. One day, you will accept this, pick a new name, and start your new life as a woman."

She pointed at the makeup table. It was fully

stocked with brushes, bottles and items Ben couldn't recognize. There was also a tablet computer. "You are going to need a lot of practice to catch up to other girls your age, I downloaded some tutorials to get you started. Have your face on when you come down to eat." She left the room. Ben staggered backward and collapsed onto the bed. He pulled the fake breasts out of his bra and began to weep.

Ben lay on the bed and tried to convince himself that his Mother had been lying about the injection. A few hours later he was suddenly struck with intense abdominal cramps that felt like someone was rearranging his organs. To his horror, he realized that was exactly what was going on, his mother had told the truth. Deep inside him, he was already growing a uterus and ovaries. As soon as he grasped what was going on, he ran to the bathroom and threw up. After he was done he washed his mouth out, trying not to look at the boy in a dress in the mirror. He went back to his "new" room, fell into the flowery bed and cried until he fell asleep.

By morning, he noticed that his body hair was thinner and his chest was tender. His mother gave him space but left strict instructions on a note stuck to his makeup mirror on what he was to wear if he wanted breakfast. That day, Ben refused to leave his room.

Ben's attempted hunger strike clashed with the

raging changes underway inside him and by the third day hunger won and he was smoothing his skirt under his growing behind as he sat to eat.
Every day after, as he got into that day's outfit, he would notice more changes. The cramps were pretty constant, his bones ached, he could no longer get an erection and his black hair had turned dirty blond and now reached his shoulders. His mother began to send him tutorials on how to braid, bun, and style his hair.
He would hear the phone ring, and his mother say that he was not available. He knew his voice was changing, and he was thankful to not have to talk to anyone. He also knew that the day would come soon, when he would have to face the world as the girl he was becoming.
The day he woke to find that he filled his bra without padding and that his testicles had retreated up into his body, leaving only a tiny nub of his shrunken penis, he refused to eat and spent the day crying in his room.
The next day, when he came down, he realized that he was now shorter than his mother. "It's almost done now, isn't it?" he asked. The soft breathy voice still surprised him every time he used it.
"Yes dear. You're..." She paused. "You're a very pretty girl"
Ben slammed his eyes shut and went back to his room ashamed. Sarah was a pretty girl! Not him! He was supposed to be a handsome man who fucked pretty girls! He should have been furious

at being called a pretty girl, but part of him was happy to hear it and he hated himself for that!

The next night, when he went to pee, he found nothing to hold onto, just a gap in the crease that had once run down the center of his now vanished scrotum. Resigned, he sat to pee. When he wiped, the crease came apart, opening his labia for the first time, unveiling a fully formed clitorus and vagina.

Ben brushed his now slender and delicate fingers over this new opening for a moment and then spun around to throw up.

Ben was all girl now and she spent the night crying and thinking.

The next morning, she asked her mother. "When you were pregnant, did you and Dad have a girl's name picked out?" Ben was wearing a black dress, mourning the boy who had vanished last night.

"We did." her mother said. "Isabella"

"Then, for him, I'll be Isabella" She replied, "Bella for short."

Isabella's mother smiled.

Bella shook her head. "I don't forgive you! But.. I can't hide forever!"

For the first time, Isabella faced the world as a girl as they went to the courthouse to make her transition official. When they got home, her mother turned on the news. As images of conflict and burning buildings flashed across the screen, the reporters announced a formal declaration of war. Both women watched the news in numb shock. Bella held her mother's hand as reporters talked about the announcement of a nation wide draft.

"It's going to get worse." Bella's mother almost whispered and squeezed Bella's hand.

As angry as Bella was about what her mother had done to her, the war brought life into perspective. Most of the male friends Bella had in school were drafted in the opening weeks so Bella never had to face them as a girl and Sarah was just as happy to have a new bestie even if she had lost a boyfriend.

Bella couldn't hate her Mother forever. In the weeks after her transformation Bella constantly leaned on her to explain many new aspects of being a girl. Especially after the first month when new abdominal pains signaled the arrival of Bella's first period.

Bella was lying on the couch with her knees pulled up and a hot-pad on her belly watching TV with her Mom and Sarah when the first phone calls came in on the 'gossip web" Sarah had included Bella on when she declared her "one of the girls".

There had been a battle, and Philip, who had been Ben's friend since grade school, was dead.

Bella barely had time to digest this when more messages came in. Sam, Robert, Dean, Chuck, all boys Ben had graduated with all died within hours of each other.

Sarah and Bella hugged and wept for their fallen friends when Bella looked over Sarah's shoulder at her mother who was watching them with sympathy and what Bella realized was relief.

Bella's mother worked for the Defense Department. She would have known better than most what was coming.

"Mom?" Bella asked. Unable to say more in front of Sarah.

"It's awful." Her mother replied. "I wouldn't be able to survive losing a child."

Bella took a deep breath, hugged Sarah tighter and mouthed two words to her mother. "Thank you."

The Girly Drink

1, Potion

John stopped on the broken sidewalk in front of a row of benches where a number of eclectically dressed people sat smoking, browsing their phones or chatting quietly. He looked up at the sign that displayed an upside down top hat and the words "Mad Hatter Tattoo" then looked down at his phone at the email he had received the day before. This was the right address, but he was not looking for a Tattoo parlor. He pushed the door open and stepped inside. The waiting area was a collection of old couches, all occupied. A table sat in the middle stacked with binders. Each binder had an artist's name on the cover with samples of their work inside.

"Do you have an appointment?" asked the woman behind the counter in a voice deeper than John expected. She was dressed in a black frilly top with a black mini skater skirt over black and white striped stockings. She had a silver nose ring and blue-green hair in a bob cut. She pointed at the waiting room. "I think we are full up on walk-ins if you don't have an appointment but you can come back tomorrow, and see if we have a slot."

John looked around for a minute blinking and then

shook his head. "No.. I, uh, I'm here to see Mr. Victor Raken?"
"Oh." The girl sighed. "Straight through to the back, the door next to the bathroom," she said, pointing past the half-door that led into an open space where customers lay on tables or reclined in chairs while artists worked with whirring needle drivers.
"Oh, uh, thank you." John said but the girl had already forgotten him. He found the latch on the backside of the door and passed through.
A woman in a black tank top with long wavy hair looked up from the drawing of a dragon she was doing on a fat man's back. John just shrugged and pointed at the door. "Raken," he said.
The woman laughed. "Good luck!" Her statement seemed to have an edge to it that bothered John for some reason.
He made his way through the parlor and put his hand on the door.
He did not turn the knob, or pull, or push, but now he was standing in what looked like a suburban basement rec-room. The walls were old wood-panel. The carpet was a thick orange shag. A fruit bowl light fixture hung from a chain over a couch and coffee table in front of a wide-screen projection TV. In the corner was a beat up red recliner where an older man with close-cut gray hair and a matching beard. He wore a black and red robe and pajama pants with brown slippers. He glanced up at John and smiled wide.

"You must be Jonathan! So nice to meet you!"

"Uh..." John stammered. He turned around and looked behind him. There was only a bookcase and a drink caddy against the panel wall. To his left, a set of stairs covered in the same orange shag carpet disappeared into the floor above. "Where? How? What?"

"Dimensional door. I had it put in during Covid so I didn't have to leave the house to ply my trade. If you feel a tingle, that's because the door scraped off any bacteria or virus you had on your clothes or skin when you passed through."

"Oh.." John said. "Handy." His brain felt like it wanted to jump out of his ear.

"Now you know," Mr. Raken said.

"Know what?" John asked.

"Walking to the shop today, you told yourself that I was probably a kook and you were only curious." He shrugged at the room. "Now you know I'm the real thing!"

"A Wizard," John said in disbelief. "An honest to God Wizard?"

"In the flesh." Mr. Raken picked up a glass of brown liquid and let the ice tinkle against the sides for a moment before taking a sip. "Have a seat!"

John glanced at the corduroy couch and then back at the strange man. His heart was racing with terror. He glanced up the stairs.

"Won't do you any good!" The man said. "I mean, the stairs will take you to the house, and the door will take you outside. But it's 1986 out there! You

won't be born for another quarter century!"
"1986?" John's mouth was dry. He staggered over to the couch and collapsed. "I time traveled?"
"Some of the best TV of all time!" Raken said. "I mean you can get a bunch of it on DVD now, but not the full experience with the commercial breaks. Did you know, in April, ABC is gonna air a unique version of Superman 3 with scenes that don't show up on any DVD or VHS copies?"
"You time traveled for Superman?" John was having trouble keeping up.
"NO!" Mr. Raken scoffed. "That would be ridiculous!"
"Ah," "said John.
"I time traveled to watch the very special Punky Brewster about the Challenger explosion." Raken drained the rest of his glass. "You want a drink?" he asked.
"I think I need one," John replied.
"Good man!" Ranken said as his chair loudly clanked, propelling him into a standing position. He then made his way to the drink tray and started fiddling with bottles. "So you want a love potion?" he asked.
"Uh.." John could feel his cheeks going flush, he was suddenly embarrassed. "Yeah, I guess that's why I'm here. There is this girl, and I finally have a date with her. Her name is Jane, and she is just... amazing."
"John and Jane?" Mr. Raken set the bottle and glass down, turned and looked at John. "Good God, your

name's not Doe is it?"
"Uh, no. It's Kowalski,"he said.
Mr. Raken turned back to the drink tray. "Almost as bad." He hefted a bottle of something blue that seemed to glow. "Too bad, I can't mix love potions."
"Oh." John sighed. "I just thought about the dimensional door and the time travel..."
"Physical world!" Mr. Raken said. "I can do what I want with the physical world!" He handed John a glass of brown liquid with ice in it. "That's some good Kentucky Bourbon from 1919, just bottled yesterday."
"Uh, I thought you said it was 1986?" John looked at the glass in his hand.
"The bourbon doesn't know that!" Mr. Raken exclaimed and then tipped back his own glass, draining it all. "Delicious!" He turned back to the drink cart and got to mixing again.
"So, uh.. If you can't make a love potion..." John paused. He had explained all this in the email exchange. This was all a waste of time. His irritation finally broke through the disorientation "Why did you call me down here?"
"To help you with your problem!" Mr. Raken said.
"But you just said you couldn't," John countered.
"I just said I couldn't change her heart, not without her consent. I can, however, offer you a physical solution, and if YOU consent I can do more than that!" Mr Raken opened a jar of something that seemed to be moving.
"Physical solution?" John asked.

"Are you Jane's dream lover?" Mr. Raken asked as he turned to face John again. This time he held a round bottle with a narrow top.

John shook his head. "I'm out of her league. She has always dated the sports stars and straight-A preppy boys. I think she just agreed to this date because she feels sorry for me."

Mr. Raken nodded. "And if you could become one of those guys, I mean physically and mentally, Would you give up who you are to become Jane's dream?"

John looked down at his glass and swirled it listening to the ice jingle. He took a large swallow. The drink was both harsh and sweet, burning his throat but leaving a nice aftertaste. "Mr. Raken, I'm a 25 year old loser who dropped out of college to play video games and fix computers. I've run the numbers. There is no world where I ever make enough to own a house, or live alone. So, if I could be one of those guys Jane usually dates, I'd do it with or without her!" He swallowed the rest of his drink. Introspection hurts.

"Very well!" Mr. Raken said. He turned and added a red ball to the bottle. It instantly dissolved. He pushed a cork stopper into the bottle and then set it in front of John on the coffee table. "Drink that, in her presence, and as you spend time with her, it will transform you into her ideal mate, physically, and mentally, but beware!" He paused, causing John to look from the bottle back up to him. "There is no going back! Magic like this shuffles the deck, there is no way to unshuffle it."

John looked down at the bottle; his mind wanted to doubt what Mr. Raken said but the room around him told him otherwise. He took a deep breath, reached out and grasped the bottle. "Ok. What do I owe you?"

Mr. Raken smiled wide. "Chaos is its own reward."

"Oh.." John said, a little afraid.

"Yeah, that sounded more creepy than I intended as soon as I said it. Just give Bree at the front desk $250. And remind her that my offer still stands"

John didn't have time to respond before he found himself falling onto his ass in the Tattoo parlor.

"Oh wow! Are you okay?" exclaimed the artist from the nearest table.

John looked around in shock and then down at the still sealed bottle in his hand. "Yeah!" he announced, pulling himself back to his feet. "I'm okay"

He staggered a couple steps past the tables and then off the floor, and back to the desk. "Are you Bree?" He asked the girl.

"Yeah!" She answered.

"I'm supposed to give you $250 and tell you his offer still stands." John said.

Bree took the card from John and ran the sale through before handing back his card and a receipt for "touch ups."

"Yeah, he keeps saying that, but some stuff you gotta do for yourself." Bree answered.

John scrunched his brow in confusion. "Do what?"

Bree looked at the bottle in John's hand for a moment and then shook her head. "Blue huh? Good luck with that!" She turned away from John and went back to her phone.

John walked out and checked his phone. He would be picking Jane up in 2 hours.

2, Jane

Jane bit her lower lip nervously as Sydny, her best friend since grade school and roommate, silently finished applying the top coat to Jane's nails.

"Honestly, Jane," Sydney said at last "I was wondering how long it would take you to figure it out."

"You knew?" Jane exclaimed.

"I've known you since 2nd grade! Of course I knew!" She replied.

"But I've been dating guys! I never…" Jane began.

"Hold up!" Sydney cut her off. "You may have dated the who's who of the hot guys around here, but you NEVER looked at any of them the way you looked at Summer Williams all senior year."

"Oh God, you noticed that?" Jane blushed.

Sydney nodded. "Drool's not a good look for you"

"Did she notice?" Jane asked. "Oh God!"

"Relax!" Sydney said. "I don't think she saw a thing! You know she was completely devoted to Brad. I heard they got married right after graduation. She is doing that whole trad wife thing, completely submissive. Kind of kinky in a church-girl way"

"If only…" Jane said.

"What, you want a Stepford wife?" Sydney scoffed.

"That's a bigger shock than you coming out as a lesbian. I thought you were Miss. Feminist!"
"There is nothing wrong with voluntary submission. To have a girl who trusts me and devotes herself to me like that would be amazing. A doting wife in an A-line dress taking care of the kids and waiting to cheer me up when I got home! " Jane said with a dreamy voice.
"So you still want kids?" Sydney asked.
Jane smiled shyly, "Yeah, I still want kids. I'm just not sure about the pregnancy and labor part."
"Maybe you can talk Miss Right into doing that for you." Sydney offered.
"Yup, that's how I want her, barefoot, pregnant, submissive and girly! But, since I'm a woman too, it wouldn't be patriarchal or sexist!" she added.
Both girls laughed.
FInally Sydney caught her breath. "So what's with this date with this John guy then? If you're not into guys..."
"It's not that I'm not into guys! I just like women... better" Jane said. "John is sweet and he asked me out like 100 times."
"Last act of mercy?" Sydney asked.
"Not just that!" Jane replied. "I always choose guys based on what I thought people expected me to want, not what I wanted. Maybe I'm not a Lesbian, maybe I have just picked the wrong guys for the wrong reason. I mean, the bedroom stuff was always fun. I like sex with guys."
"So he is an experiment?" Sydney asked.

"Something like that." Jane replied.

"Well, your experiment is going to be here in about thirty minutes and you need to get your face on." Sydney said flatly.

John was right on time. The doorbell rang at 2pm on the dot.

Jane took one last look into the mirror. Her blond hair was in a pull through waterfall braid that Sydney had done. She wore small dangling silver earrings and a purple satin sleeveless halter top body-hugging mini dress. It was warm so she had skipped tights, and stood on modest 2" pumps.

The winged liquid eyeliner Sydney had done looked fantastic and Jane wondered if she had gone overboard for a date that would be going nowhere.

"Consider it practice for your first date with a girl." Sydney had said. The thought put Jane's nerves at ease. Knowing that she had no expectations with John, let her feel more free to enjoy herself than she would have otherwise.

She opened the door and smiled at John with his close cropped hair, Khaki pants and red button down shirt. She realized that she was the same height as him and debated switching out for flats.

"Hello," Jane said. "Thanks for picking me up!"

"I'm happy too." John cast a nervous glance over his shoulder. "You look amazing!"

"Thank you" Jane blushed.

"Shall we?" John motioned out to the sidewalk.

"Are we going to be doing a lot of walking?" Jane

asked.
"Uh I thought we could stroll by the canal." John answered.
It gave Jane the perfect excuse. "In that case, wait here. Heels are a bad choice." She scurried back into her apartment toward her room.
"Back so soon?" Sydney asked.
"Shut up!" Jane replied as she kicked her pumps off and slipped on a pair of black ballet shoes.
As she came back to the door, she saw that John was now a little taller than her and that he was holding an empty antique bottle.
"What's that?" she asked.
"Oh..." John had a guilty look. "Uh.. my friend made his own blackberry brandy. Just a bit of liquid courage." He shrugged.
"Should I drive?" Jane asked.
"No." John shook his head. "It was pretty weak and, uh.. I have a rideshare anyway. Sorry."
Jane felt sorry for the boy. "Oh, that's ok." She looked over his shoulder at the waiting blue SUV with a strange man behind the wheel. "It'll give us time to talk." She took John's hand and led him to the car. His hand felt rough and calloused. Jane remembered that he worked on computers all day.
"Your hands are pretty tough for a computer guy," she said as he climbed into the back seat beside her.
"I do woodcarving as a hobby," John said. "The tools take their toll I guess." He stroked his palm with his finger.
"I like it" Jane lied and took his hand in hers.

"Manly hands."

John blushed. "Thanks," he said then added "You look nice."

Jane ran her free hand up the side of her leg. "I just shaved them, may as well show them off," she said.

"Oh man!" John said. "Shave! I must look..." he paused as he ran his hand over his chin. It was smooth and soft. He scrunched his brow. "Uhh, I thought for sure that I had..." he stopped again. On the word "had" his voice had cracked an octave higher. "..had." Still higher. He cleared his throat. "Had." It sounded deeper, but a little forced. "Uh... forgotten to shave"

Jane could tell that John was making an effort to sound manly.

"Is everything alright?" she asked.

John put his hand on his throat and seemed a little confused by what he felt there. "I uh.. Must have something in my throat." he said. His voice was not as resonant as it had been at the door. He cleared his throat again. This time the sound was more dainty, almost a squeak. "Weird."

"I wouldn't worry." Jane said. "Could be your friend's brandy"

"Sorry," John said and then covered his mouth with his fingers, embarrassed. Understanding lit his face and he smiled. "Must be!" He said confidently this time in a voice that was almost feminine.

"So what do you carve?" Jane asked.

John smiled, he loved to talk about woodcarving

and began to talk in depth about his rocking chair project. It was the first piece of practical furniture he had tried.

By the time they arrived at the Canal district, despite John's higher voice, they were talking with ease. As they descended the stairs to the canal, Jane noticed something was odd, she couldn't place it. John seemed to take no notice and was listening intently to her as she tried to claim that she had no hobbies of her own.

"That can't be true," John said. "What do you spend time doing when you have nothing to do?"

"Well, I read," Jane said.

"What about?"

In Jane's mind's eyes she saw her e-reader library full of Sapphic romance novels. "Mostly junk I guess."

"Don't say that!" John pleaded. "If you enjoy it, it can't be junk." A lock of hair fell in front of John's face which surprised Jane. It was not as close cropped as she had thought; it must have been an illusion in how he had styled it.

John brushed it aside and then took Jane's hand in his own. This time his hand was warm and soft against her and she smiled down at him. He looked up at her wide-eyed. "You know you are beautiful," he said. "I always thought so."

Jane bent down and kissed him. Something tickled her mind about this. His lips were soft and full. He opened his mouth and let Jane push her tongue in. She reached up and stroked his smooth jaw back and brushed against his hair.

Jane could feel herself blushing as she stepped back from their kiss. She had never felt this way about a boy before, but no boy had ever looked at her with such devotion like he just had. His brown eyes were so round and large and expressive with lashes that seemed impossibly long.

She smirked at him. He smiled back, with full thick red lips.

"I never thought I would get to kiss you," John said. He reached out and took her hand again. "The Bar in this hotel has the best view and the best mixed drinks in the city," he explained as he led her to the entry. As he passed through the revolving door, Jane suddenly realized what had been confusing her.

Wasn't he taller than her when the date started?

3, Unexpected Girl

John knew the potion was working almost as soon as he had swallowed it. He could feel a tingle and shift inside his body. So far he had realized that Jane must like clean shaven men with soft hands. He wasn't crazy about the voice, but he couldn't argue with the results. Jane had kissed him! That's what mattered. Now that he had spent some time with her in person, he realized that she was much taller than he remembered. He also realized that she was more important to him than he had known. She was everything to him and she had kissed him. He was so happy he could scream, but he had to play it cool, stick to the plan for the afternoon and that meant drinks at the Westward Royal bar.

The elevator took them up to the rooftop and they emerged into a quiet din of the rooftop bar. Remembering that he enjoyed his drink earlier in the day, he ordered another bourbon for himself and a Mojito for Jane.

"How did you find this place?" Jane asked as she looked around in wonder at the white marble finish and fire features which turned the space into a hip yet cozy retreat.

John blushed. "I was between jobs and worked as a window cleaner for a bit," he said. He pointed at the floor to ceiling window overlooking the state capitol outside. "I was washing that pane right there, suspended hundreds of feet in the air and I thought, one day, I will take the most beautiful girl I know to that bar." He put his hand on Jane's "And here we are."

Jane smiled, blushed, and pushed a lock of hair over her ear.

The bartender returned, setting their drinks on the bar and taking John's card. Down the bar a party in office attire erupted into obnoxious laughter.

"Do you want to go out to the balcony?" John asked. "It's quieter."

"Sounds like a good idea" Jane replied and the two moved out into the open air that looked down on the river.

John sipped his drink and nearly coughed. It seemed harsher than the one this afternoon had been. He assumed the lack of time travel selection had something to do with it. He turned to cover his facial expression, set his glass on the table, cleared his throat and turned back to Jane who was much closer than he had expected. She caught his face in her hands, bent down and kissed him again. John, wanting to reassert his manliness, wrapped his arms around her and tried to cup the back of her head in his hand but it seemed awkward. He cursed when Jane pulled away and looked out over

the river.
She smiled, shook her head and laughed to herself.
"What is it?" John asked.
"I'm just, uh, surprised," she answered then sighed. "God! I'm awful!"
"I don't think so," John answered.
"I never intended to kiss you," she said. "Except for a peck to say good night." She turned to John. "I don't know what came over me."
John smiled, "Maybe we just fit."
"That's what's so surprising! Earlier tonight, I had been all but sure that I was a lesbian." She said, "At least I thought that I was. I even came out to my roommate! I spent a long time trying to pretend I wasn't but... I have never felt attraction for men. Until you, tonight, and I don't know." She paused and pounded her hand on the railing "I just don't know! I was so sure! I thought I knew what I wanted. But then you come along and now I'm all confused again!" She sighed and sipped her drink. "This would be so much easier if you were a girl".
John blinked for a few moments, unable to fully understand what she had just said. The potion was clearly working. She had initiated both kisses, but how could it be turning him into her ideal man if she wasn't attracted to men? Slowly the obvious answer dawned on him, he grew hot. He felt sweat bead on his brow. Mr. Rankin didn't say "Ideal man" Mr. Rankin had said, "Ideal mate." Jane had just said she would like him better if he was a girl! His breath was short and he looked down at his

soft, delicate hands, the nails had grown since the night began and acquired a pink solid color. They were painted! Mr. Rankin's potion was turning John into Jane's ideal girl! There suddenly didn't seem to be any air out on the balcony.

"I…" John stepped back. "I need to use the bathroom" he said, then spun around and walked quickly into the bar, past the tables and through the door marked "Men" hoping it still applied to him. The person in the mirror shocked him. It sort of looked like him, if he was shorter, thinner with softer jawbones and longer hair. What had been a close cut right part was now a wavy cascade down the right side of his face. His eyes went wide and he quickly ran into a stall and opened his fly.

Everything was still where it was supposed to be. He was pleased at first to find that his penis seemed thicker and longer in his hand, but he realized that his hand was smaller than when he drank the potion, he had no way of knowing how much that had changed. He took a deep breath and slid his hand up his shirt. He closed his eyes in despair as he found his chest to be softer and a little fuller than when the day had begun.

Rankin had said that these changes were irreversible. His height, his hands, his voice, and his chest would be like this from now on, but he could leave right now. Get away and stay away from Jane and nothing more would happen! The smart thing to do would be to go down the elevator right now and get on with his life.

But this was Jane. The girl of his dreams. The girl he wanted to spend his life with! He couldn't just strand her like that!

John shook his head. That was crazy! Maybe that was the potion. Nothing could be trusted now, and he had to get out!

But Jane needed him, he had to make sure she got home safe! He could never abandon her like that! She was too important to him, even if it did cost him a little more masculinity!

John looked in the mirror, "Ok, but, don't be rude. Just tell her there is an emergency, take her back downstairs and get her a new rideshare" He pulled out his phone and keyed up the app. A driver would be there in five minutes. How much more could change in five minutes? He pushed open the door and almost hit Jane in the face.

"John! I was beginning to think you left me behind!" she said with a soft smile.

"Ohh, sorry!" He held up his phone. "Family emergency, I'm going to have to cut our night short, I'm afraid."

Jane gave a bemused smile. "I understand. You don't...thank you I suppose."

"For what?" John asked.

Jane shrugged. "For trying to make it seem like it wasn't about what I just told you."

"Oh Jane, no!" John said. "There really is an emergency!" It hurt his heart to lie to her. If it had to go on much longer, he didn't think he could keep it up!

She didn't look convinced.

John hated that look on her face, loneliness and rejection. How dare he harm her? He looked down at his phone to stop seeing it. "Ride's almost here! The bar has my card number so let's just go."

"Ok," sighed Jane and headed toward the elevator without waiting for John.

A voice in John's head told him he could get out now. Let her storm off on her own and then never see her again then the potion would do no more, but seeing her slumped shoulders, he just couldn't let her go. Despite his better judgment he raced to catch up. "Let me walk you to the car," he said as he joined her waiting for the elevator.

They could hear the party coming up before the light and the bell went off. The elevator was packed with far more people than it should have held. They were laughing and hooting and they were forever getting off and some of the women's dresses looked rather out of order. John raised his eyebrows as he looked at Jane but Jane kept her eyes forward until she stepped in and then she just looked up at the numbers.

"You know John," she said. "The irony was that you almost had me turned around. Finally I was enjoying myself with a man! I was starting to think I could make it work with you." She shook her head. "I'm a fool"

John's heart broke a little with every word she spoke. All he wanted was to make her happy. A part of him wanted to stay even knowing what that would do to him. He wanted to know what it would cost. "Jane," he said. "Describe your perfect..."

The lights cut out and the elevator jammed to a violent halt at the same time. John almost fell over. They were in pitch darkness for a moment and then amber emergency lights lit the small space. John looked to make sure Jane was ok. She had a hand out braced against the rail along the elevator wall but otherwise she was fine.

"Power outage?" He asked in exasperation. Panic was beginning to build within him. He needed to get away from Jane.

"Looks like it," Jane said. "Hope that car waits for me."

"I hope it's not a long enough wait that it matters," John said.

"Thanks," Jane replied with a hurt tone.

"No!" John turned to her. "It's not that! It's the emergency!" He turned his back and went back to pressing buttons on the dark console.

"What emergency?" Jane asked. "Like you went on a date, found out I was a lesbian, realized you weren't getting anywhere so you decided to cut your losses?"

"NO!" John said. "That's not what this is!" He pulled open the call box door and lifted the phone handle. There was a series of clicks.

"Then what is it?" Jane demanded.

"Hello?" Came a voice from the handset.

John held up his hand to Jane and replied "Yes, we

are stuck in the elevator and need to get to the ground floor."

"Yes ma'am" said the voice causing a wave of fury to wash over John. "Building services is aware of your situation. Unfortunately we are experiencing a mechanical failure. Building services have called the elevator repair company but it may be several hours before they can arrive. The hotel will, of course, compensate you with a complimentary room for your inconvenience."

"No!" John pleaded into the handset, " I need to get out of this box!" He glanced at Jane in terror. "You need to get us off."

"I'm sorry ma'am, you are between floors, there is no safe way to get you out of that car. Please make yourself comfortable and we will be happy to compensate you once repairs are complete." There was a click and the line went dead.

John smacked the handset into the cradle several times and then left it hanging as he slumped against the wall. "Oh God!" he muttered.

"Is there someone you can call?" Jane asked.

John turned. She was almost hovering over him, he stepped back into the corner away from her. "What?"

"Your emergency," she said. "Is there anyone you need to call to let them know you can't come?"

John shook his head and shifted down the wall farther from Jane. His insides felt weird.

"What the hell?" Jane said. "Your hair!" She reached for John's head and ran her fingers through the blond hair that now cascaded down past his face. "It was brown...and you were taller." She grabbed John's hand and ran her thumb over his soft palm. She turned it over and looked at his pink nails. "These weren't here earlier! What is going on? What's the emergency?"

"You are," John said in his now feminine voice. "I was so excited about our date that I went to see this guy. He was uh.. magic? A wizard I guess"

"A wizard?" Jane asked incredulously. Then she looked down as John wiggled the nail lad fingers on his dainty feminine hands, she remembered the manly hands from the car. "Ok..a wizard."

"He made me a potion." He handed the empty antique bottle to Jane.

She turned it over in the faint emergency lighting. On the front was a paper label written in calligraphy "Love Potion Sixty Nine"

"It's supposed to turn me into your perfect mate." John sighed. "I thought that meant the kinds of guys you usually date, like Brad Hastings. When I found out that you preferred...." He ran his fingers through the long blond wavy hair that now fell from his head. "Well....It's working!"

"Oh God!" Jane recognized the hair. It was the same hair Summer Williams had their senior year. "My dream girl! How do we stop it?"

John stepped to the opposite corner. "We can't now. As long as I'm with you, I keep changing, mind and body, the only way to stop is to get away and never come near you again."

"Oh John." She looked around at the dark elevator. "Oh, God! I'm so sorry." She turned and pulled at the doors, nothing moved. John joined her and they each pulled, the door barely budged.

"I think I've lost strength," John lamented and slumped against the wall.

"Maybe up?" Jane asked.

"That's a movie thing." John sighed. "In the real world they are bolted shut from the outside so only emergency services can get into them"

"Well this is an emergency!" Jane said.

John grabbed at the handset. "Hello! Hello!" It was silent. He hung it up and then lifted it again. There was no tone. He looked down to see cracks in the handle. He had broken it in his temper tantrum earlier. "Fuuuuuuck!" He said.

"Maybe we should," Jane said.

John turned to look at her. "Should what?"

"Does your dick still work? I mean is it still in your pants?" Jane asked. She cringed a little at how the question sounded when she heard it out loud.

John reached down to confirm and nodded. "For now."

"Right, for now," Jane said. "If we can't get out of this elevator, it may be gone soon." She reached behind her neck and began to lower the zipper of her dress. "The least I can do is give it one...." she caught the zipper with her other hand and finished sliding it down. "Final.." She let the dress fall to her feet. She wore no bra. Her breasts were pert and round. She had black lacy boyshorts on.

"Ride" She knelt in front of him and began pulling at his belt.

John was pinned against the wall. "Jane you don't have to," he said. He could feel himself swelling against his underwear as she began to unbutton his pants and pull at his zipper. "You were just telling me..."

"It's men's personalities I don't prefer. I never minded the parts," she said. She let his pants fall and hooked her fingers to his waistband. "Maybe if I remind myself how much I like it, you'll get to keep it."

John felt a ray of hope. He'd still be a girl, but a girl with a dick at least. "Yeah... I...yeah!" he stammered.

Rather than answer, Jane wrapped her lips around his cock and began to play her tongue against the head.

John gripped the bar on the elevator wall. "Oh GOD!" he sighed. He looked down in disbelief at Jane, the girl he had dreamed of for so long, on her knees with his dick in her mouth. She took him deep, with her lips brushing the base, then slid back, her tongue tip sliding along his vein. He groaned in pleasure as the sound of suckling filled the small dark space. At last he found his voice, frail and high as it was and asked the question that terrified him. "Is it....small?"

Jane pulled her mouth away with a loud smack and wiped a stream of salvia mixed with precum from her chin. She kept his cock in her hand and looked up at him with wide eyes. "Long and hard!" she lied and licked her lips and then teased his tip with her tongue. "I want it inside me!" she said before opening wide and plunging her mouth down on it again while her hand slid down and cupped his balls. She sucked her cheeks in and focused her tongue on the ridge under his head. Even with her lips against his belly it didn't reach the back of her throat.

"Oh God!" John repeated again. This was not the first blowjob he had ever received, but it was the best. A twinge of sorrow reminded him that it could also be the last. He looked down at Jane again. This time his chest partially obscured his view. He reached up in disbelief to cup his tits. "Oh GOD!" he exclaimed once more.

Jane pulled back, paused to gently kiss the head of his cock and said "Not yet!" She pulled John's hands down from his breasts as she sat down on the elevator floor, pulling John down on top of her. "You deserve to blow your last load in a cunt!'

"Last? Load?" John asked, "You think..."

"I think that, as much as I tried, I don't think I'll miss..." She brushed her fingers across her lips. "That." She pointed at his dripping cock. "I'm sorry, but your balls have already..uh"

John grabbed his crotch. His scrotum was empty and he thought he could feel something moving inside him. "Oh shit," he said as he wrapped his hand around his hard cock as though he was going to keep it in place. He sputtered out a sob and tears rolled down his soft smooth cheeks.

“One last fuck” Jane said and brushed John’s hair aside then brushed away a tear. “Come on baby, you’re going to be my dream girl. We are going to be together forever. Even as my wife, maybe you can still be our child’s father.”

John looked at her through watery eyes in disbelief. He drew in a deep breath and felt his tits heave as he did so. They were huge, as he bent over Jane he could feel their weight pulling at him.

“Hurry! I don’t think we have much time,” she said as she lifted her butt off the floor and slid her panties off.

John moved between her legs as she opened them. She brought her knees up. He lowered himself and her hand caught his cock, guiding him into her wet opening. He slid in and she smiled. “Still long and hard!” She reassured him gently. It was smaller than most of her toys now. She had felt it shrinking in her mouth, but it was still enough to reach her g-spot at least for now. She could feel him rubbing against it inside her.

He began to thrust, slowly, rhythmically. He could feel her squirm under her. She cupped his breast and lifted it to her lips, suckling him and the sensation was mindblowing. He didn’t even realize he had sped up his thrusting as she played her tongue over the nipple. He couldn’t concentrate. He lifted up, pulling his tit from her mouth and then came down onto his elbows. His massive breasts pushed against her smaller ones.

He could feel them roll against each other as he thrust his wider hips.

She moaned and squirmed more.

He thrust harder, deeper, and faster.

She thought about the fact that this would be the last time he ever fucked a woman as a man. She thought about the fact that he would soon be her woman, beautiful, submissive and dependent on her. She thought about the fact that everything about John was reshaping to her will and more than the small cock inside her, the sense of power boiled her over into orgasm! She balled a fist and banged it against the elevator floor as she screamed in ecstasy.

He could feel her pussy clamp and spasm around his cock.

A thundering pulse came up deep from inside him. He moaned and the moan turned into a high pitched squeal and he felt his cock pulse with pleasure as warm fluid pumped into her, but this was so much more than any orgasm he had ever felt. It rushed over his body radiating out across his hips, up his belly, down his legs. He felt everything shudder and something vital and powerful was pumped out of him.

He gasped and collapsed on top of Jane. No words were spoken as Jane's arms and legs came up around him. “Don’t go,” she whispered. She wanted him inside her till the end. She wanted to feel it go.

He sighed and allowed himself to collapse into her.

"Shhhhh," Jane said, stroking John's hair.

John could feel himself growing soft inside Jane.

"I'll take care of you," Jane whispered as she kept stroking his hair. She felt him shrinking much faster now.

John felt his cock sliding out. He knew it was shrinking, but he didn't want to break his embrace with Jane. She would always be here for him. No matter what happened, she would be here.

"My sweet dream girl," Jane said. She kissed him on his cheek. "Rest in me, my darling girl" she could feel it now between them, shrinking, and then there was nothing between their bellies.

John felt a tightness between his legs. "It's gone," he whimpered. He didn't realize he had been crying till now.

"Shhh, I know sweety. I'll help you learn," Jane whispered.

John felt the tightness grow and then something split between his legs, rather than hurt, he felt tingles of pleasure as the skin parted. He sobbed. "I think it's opened. Oh god! I have a pussy!"

Jane held him tight against her and whispered. "It's ok. You're my girl and I'll look after you. Shhh. I'll take care of you. Just rest in me." She stroked John's long hair. Her arm traced down John's curvy back to a soft round ass which Jane cupped.

John believed every word and soon the two women were asleep in each other's arms.

4, The comp

As hotel guests passed through the lobby on the way to breakfast, the elevator marked "Out of order" finally opened on the ground floor and two women emerged. One wore a satin minidress, the other, an oversized men's red button down that strained against her massive breasts and Khakis that had their cuffs rolled up several times. The woman in the dress crossed directly to the front desk, while the other woman stood back shyly glancing round as though feeling hunted.

"You promised us a complimentary room for being stuck in your elevator, I think we are due a suite!"

"Yes ma'am," said the overweight man behind the desk. "I think I can arrange for a voucher toward a future stay... "

"No," Jane interrupted, "Your best suite! Checking in, NOW!"

The man took a breath. "Miss, check in is not until 2pm!"

"We have been stuck in your elevator since Six PM!" Jane retorted. "Thirteen hours of torment for us is worth a hell of a lot more than..." She looked at the clock "Seven hours of inconvenience for you!"

He opened his mouth as though wanting to argue,

saw her face, and then looked down and began tapping at his keyboard. After a few moments he said "Yes ma'am, our Jefferson Suite is available immediately. That has a King sized bed, a separate living space as well as an extra large Jacuzzi tub.

"Perfect!" Jane said. "We'll take it, and a room service menu!"

John was still in shock as Jane led her into the room. She let Jane lead her to a couch and then sat down. She looked at her hands again. The nails were now long and pink at the end of slender delicate fingers. Her hand drifted up to her hair, blond, wavy and long, cascading down to her mid torso. She traced her nails through it and came down to rest on her breast as it pushed out, straining the buttons of her shirt. Her hand cupped under her right breast and hefted it, feeling the weight as it pulled at her side and shoulder. It was real. She looked up at Jane with a look of loss.

"Sorry." Jane said "I guess I like big tits" She was still standing and holding her purse

"I'm a girl," John said in stunned shock. She stood back up and walked over to a floor to ceiling mirror that was bolted inexplicably by the dinning table. She brushed her hair with her fingers again and then pulled up her pants so they pressed against her flat crotch. She let them droop loose as they were and then pressed her right hand between her legs. "I have ...."

"Yes." Jane said. "I'm sorry."

John turned to her with pleading eyes. “You’re going to help me?”

Jane took the frightened girl into her arms and pulled her close. “Always,” she said and kissed her ear. “I want to show you how wonderful it is to be a woman.”

John trusted her and felt relief again at her words. “Just tell me what to do,” she said.

Jane stepped back. “I need to step out! You need clothes, and other things! I’ll be back by lunch time! I promise!” She looked John over and then put her hands around John’s waist. “Size 2 maybe....” She put her hands on John’s breasts. “Yikes! E cup?” She shook her head. “I’m so sorry about those.”

“Do they make you happy?” John asked.

Jane smiled and nodded. “Yeah...they look real good on you.”

John nodded, “then I’ll love them too,” she said. “The potion says I have to.” She let out a deep sigh.

Jane stepped back and held her hand up next to John’s face. “A shade lighter,” she said and moved towards the door. “Sit down, watch TV. Don’t dwell on it! I’ll be back.” She opened the door, “And don’t discover the Jacuzzi jets without me!” She stepped out and let the door close.

John was standing in the hotel suite alone. Her feet were swimming in her shoes so she stepped out of them and noticed how baggy her socks were. She pulled them off to discover dainty little feet the nails painted the same sparkly pink polish as her hands. She traced her thumb over her big toe, then looked down at her breasts once more while pushing the cascade of blond hair back over her shoulder. Her button down shirt was straining over her tits and she could feel tightness with every breath, so she unbuttoned her shirt and pulled it off. Her thin white t-shirt left almost nothing to the imagination as her nipples were clearly defined in the fabric and the round globes they sat on pulled the fabric around them. John took a deep breath, closed her eyes and pulled the shirt up over her head then guided her locks through the neck-hole before letting it fall to the floor.

Her breasts were real! In the dark elevator, and then under the fabric, out of direct sight, she had not fully absorbed that they were there. They could have been padding or a costume. Now that she was topless, looking down at the supple smooth skin as it sloped from her thin shoulder out to the nipple and then curved under and out of her sight they had a reality to them. She traced that slope of skin with her finger and as her nail brushed the areole she shivered. They were more sensitive than she could have believed. She stroked the nipple a few more times and rolled it between her fingers. She felt an electric shiver through her body and a moisture between her legs. Realizing what she felt, she froze "I have a pussy," she said to herself.

She returned to the full length mirror. When she

saw the petite beautiful blond girl with massive tits in the mirror she felt a spark of longing and was reminded again of the slick wetness she felt in a place she should not have. She opened her pants and let them fall. Her tighty-whitey briefs were baggy and had no bulge in front. With a resignation to her loss, she pushed them down below her wide hips and they fell past her slender smooth hairless legs to the floor.

Jane apparently liked her girls clean-shaven. Her slender waist flared out to her hips, but in the middle was smooth skin from her belly button down to the two hairless lips that enclosed the slit where her cock and balls had once been. Again, seeing it, made it far more real than she was prepared for. She was a woman, sexy, petite, and absurdly proportioned.

Her hand went down to the slit and brushed over the lips. She pressed her palm against the flatness that once held her penis and, almost without thinking, she curved her middle finger so that it slid between her outer lips to brush the entry beneath. She could feel the wetness, slick and warm, her own lubricant made by an organ she did not possess yesterday. Her heart raced. She looked herself in the eye and shook her head as though trying to warn herself against what she was about to do as her finger brushed the threshold and then felt the warm nub of her clit for the very first time. The sensation was like a woman's tongue on the head of her dick only magnified. Her knees almost buckled in shock.

She stroked it again. "Holy shit," she exclaimed in a breathy voice. She began to rub it back and forth. She put out her left hand to brace herself against the wall and stared at herself in the mirror. As she rubbed, her hips seemed to gyrate on their own causing her tits to sway beneath her. She was so fucking hot to look at! She rubbed harder and felt pressure building inside her. She was a girl now, fingering herself, she was the girl in the mirror with the blond hair and giant tits rubbing her pussy, the thought terrified her and turned her on at the same time. She squealed! She had never squeaked in her life, but she had never been a girl rubbing her own clit before either. Her whole body was tingling and throbbing. She needed release but it would not come. She concentrated on the sensation between her legs. She tried to pretend the hot girl in the mirror was not her.

Her mind interrupted her to ask how narcissistic it would be to get off to herself especially in the middle of this crisis in her life. This calmed the mood and she slowed, frustrated, but her body still surged. She still needed to be released.

She resumed the rubbing and stood up straight grabbing her left tit in her left hand and rolling her nipple between her fingers. She lifted it to her lips and moistened it, then went back to rubbing it with her fingers. The surging pleasure grew more and more but would not crash. At last her finger slipped off her clit and brushed through the threshold. Her eyes went wide as she looked at herself. She was really about to do this! She pushed her finger up inside herself. The alien sensation inside her made her moan. Her hand left her breast and swam in space behind her. She backed up to the couch and fell over the arm, her legs in the air. She plunged her middle finger in deep and then slid out. Suddenly she crossed a point that made her knees straighten! She rubbed it harder, she needed more! She pushed her ring finger up into herself, feeling herself wrap around her fingers, a sensation of fullness combined with the waves of pleasure from the tips of her fingers against her newly found G-spot.

The wave finally crashed! She screamed. In the daze that followed she slid her fingers out of herself and looked at them, dripping, sticky, she brought them to her lips and sucked them dry. She loved the taste of her own pussy. She was sure that Jane's would taste even better. She hoped she would come back soon. She wanted to share this with Jane. She never knew women could feel so much pleasure! She wanted to give Jane the pleasure she just gave herself. She wanted to give everything to her! Serving Jane would make all of this worthwhile. She may have lost her manhood, and with it, her job and her whole life before today, but, if she had Jane she could be happy, even as a girl.

She would be Jane's girl. She would do whatever Jane said and dedicate herself to making Jane happy.

The phone rang, startling John. She rolled off the couch and picked up the receiver. "Hello,"she said, then cringing again at her new girly voice.

"Hey! It's Jane!" Came the response "Have you put any thought into a new name? I assume you're not going to go on being called John with how you look."

John was stumped. "Uhhhh," she looked up at the flush naked beauty in the mirror. Jane was right, that girl could not go around calling herself John.

"I uh… I hadn't thought about it."

"Oh well, no rush." Jane sounded disappointed and the thought of upsetting her devastated John.

"No, we should pick a name," she quickly added. "What's the name of your dream girl?"

"No. I can't pick it for you, it's your name!" Jane said.

The blond girl in the mirror needed a name. She also was beginning to understand the rules of this game. "I think we both know that neither of us will be happy with any name unless it is the name you want me to have."

"God, I'm so sorry!" Jane said again. The remorse in her voice stung.

"Don't, I chose to drink the potion. It's what I get for cheating. A lifetime of happiness with you."

"But not as yourself!" Jane said.

"I chose that too." She sighed and looked into her own wide blue eyes in the mirror as her free hand cupped her breast. Now, may I please know my name?".

"Audrey," Jane said.

Audrey nodded to herself in the mirror. It fit perfectly as she knew it would. She should have known. That girl in the mirror was always named Audrey. "Thank you," Audrey said.

"I'll be back soon," Jane replied and hung up.

Audrey took a deep breath and accepted who she was. She would be Jane's good girl and that wouldn't be so bad.

5, Jane and Audrey

Audrey had a lot of time to herself as she waited for Jane to return. She considered masturbating again, but what she really wanted was Jane. She thought about the hot-tub, but Jane had told her not to discover the jets without her and she would hate to disobey.

She turned on the TV, standing naked in the sitting room flipping channels until she found an old '80s crime drama.

Rather than try and wrestle her tits back into her too-small T-shirt, she just pulled her red button down around her shoulders. She left the top three buttons undone to reduce pressure, leaving her cleavage out in the open. Then she picked up her khakis and her wallet fell out.

She picked it up and hesitated before opening it. She would see her old face. John's face. The face of a man who would never be seen again. Who would look for him? Should she send a letter to John's parents? What would she write?

She opened the wallet and then dropped it almost instantly as though it was too hot to touch. It landed open on the floor and the face on the Driver's license stared up at her. It was the face she had just seen in the mirror. The face of a petite blond girl next to the name "Audrey Kowalski".

She picked the wallet back up. It wasn't just her body! Her credit cards,student ID and even her grocery discount card had all been amended with her new name. In a way, this was more surprising than her own transformation. Her body was just her body, a single item in the universe. These cards are all tied to networks that spanned the world. If Rankin had changed these, he had changed the fundamental universe. "Shuffle the deck indeed," she whispered. Now she knew why it would be so hard to undo.

Audry picked up her discarded underwear and was about to step back into them when she paused. The waist band seemed huge in her dainty hands now that she lacked anything for it to support. She dropped them with a sigh. Those were men's clothes, and she had no business wearing them anymore.

She found a pair of soft robes hanging in the bathroom. The smaller of the two seemed to fit her well enough, though she didn't like how much of her new cleavage was visible even when she tried to wrap herself snugly. Her tits pushed out so far in front of her that the robe just could only do so much. She finally decided that Jane would enjoy the show, so she accepted her appearance and returned to the main room with the intention of collapsing on the couch in self pity.

On the way, her eyes fell on the clock over the

kitchen stove. They never made it to dinner last night and Jane had not had breakfast yet. She would be hungry when she got back. At first Audry was going to call for room service, but once she had the desk on the line, she instead asked for groceries, eggs, bacon, vegetables and orange juice. As a man, she rarely cooked, but now, she felt inspired. A part of her suspected that this was the potion at work once more, but that knowledge didn't change the fact that she desperately wanted to cook for Jane.

By the time Jane returned, a large gym bag over her shoulder and several shopping bags in hand, Audry had set out two place settings with fresh fruit. She poured the eggs into the pan as the door opened and smiled at her love. "Get started on your fruit. I have a feeling that you like mushrooms, peppers and swiss in your omelet," she said.

"That's right!" Jane said with surprise.

"I honestly don't know how I'm doing this." she said as she gently lifted the edge of the egg to allow the liquid to flow underneath. "I have never cooked an omelet in my life." She laid down the cheese and added the veggies on top.

Jane slumped down in front of a fruit bowl. Raspberries, blueberries, and strawberries. The exact combination she made for herself when she felt like a treat. "Omelets are my favorite," she sighed. "I'm sorry."

"Don't be!" Audry replied quickly. "It's my own

fault for drinking that thing, and cooking for you is making me happy."

Jane blushed. "Yeah... that's me too."

Audry arranged a sprig of parsley on the plate and set it in front of Jane. "You wanted a girl that could cook?"

Jane winced a little. "Sorry"

"Cooking isn't so bad," Audry replied as she returned to the kitchen and began cleaning the pans and putting items in the dishwasher.

"Cooking, cleaning, uhhh keeping house. I kinda wanted a woman who could do uhhh." Jane paused. "Women's work"

Audry looked down at the kitchen counter she was wiping clean. "Ohh. So I'm going to be June Cleaver?"

"I think the term is uhhh...Trad wife" Jane said.

"How fitting!" Audry said as she shrugged with her hands out and looked down at her massive tits.

"I'm so sorry!" Jane said again. "It was a fantasy! I didn't think I'd ever find someone who would fit it."

"Lucky you," Audry said sarcastically, "You found someone who got themselves custom tailored to it." She came around the counter and sat opposite Jane, picking at her fruit she huffed, that huff turned into a sob. She hadn't let herself cry in years! It just wasn't manly, but being manly didn't seem to matter anymore. She let herself shake as she cried for her lost manhood, her penis which she rather enjoyed, her wardrobe which was not special but still hers, her plans for her future, she cried for a life that had just closed off from her. The world of endless possibilities John still thought lay ahead of him yesterday had narrowed to one future that boy would never have expected. Audry would be a woman's housewife, that was all, forever. She imagined what that would be like and surprisingly, it didn't seem as horrible as she would have thought only a day ago. Finally Audry looked up.

Jane looked miserable, she was staring at Audry and her eyes were filled with pity. That look devastated Audry, she couldn't stand to have Jane suffer. As much as she mourned the loss of her manhood and dreaded a future in A-line dresses cooking casseroles, the idea of upsetting Jane was even worse.

"Look," she said, "Cooking apparently makes me happy now, I'm sure the rest of that stuff will too. So I get to stay home and do what I like from now on. That doesn't sound so bad." She shrugged. "I know it's the spell, but if I'm happy, does it matter why?"

"It's not you, John," Jane said. "It's what I imposed on you!"

"I'm Audry now," she replied. "But even when I was John, I wanted to make you happy. I'm sure that isn't the only thing that hasn't changed." She thought for a moment, her mind wandered to the chair she had been sanding the day before. She decided to switch to a finer grit, try and get it even smoother. "Woodworking!" she blurted "Something from before that I loved! I still love it! When I'm carving or sanding or staining something, you will know that it's something of John from before. Ok?"

Jane smiled. "Thank you, I feel better."

Audry felt a thrill of satisfaction. She had made Jane happy. That was all that mattered to her. Again, she suspected the potion, but she remembered wanting to make Jane happy before she drank it, so maybe this thought had come from her.

Once Breakfast was finished, Jane pointed to the gym bag. "I picked up some things from home, but I am not sure what may fit you. I'm taller, and you are much more...uh.. Buxom!"

"You mean I'm short and my tits are huge?" Audry asked only half jokingly. She was not thrilled about her new dimensions.

"Yeah!" Jane said as she unzipped the bag. She pulled out a brown purse. "One of my old ones but it's a start, most of our clothes don't have pockets and there is more to carry." She pulled out a smaller zipper-closed cloth bag with a flower print. "Some makeup, I'll show you how." She pulled out and held up a black midi skirt. "Stretchy waist, should fit you." She pulled out several others.

"No pants?" Audry asked, disappointed.

"Mine would be too long for you. Wait!" She reached down into her bag "I have some leggings"

Audry sighed. "Skirts it is I guess"

Jane pulled a shopping bag over. "Also!" She pulled out a sealed pack of women's panties in a variety of colors. Audry was a little disappointed to see that they were thongs. . "Underwear is not something you hand down." She reached back down again and pulled out a stack of bras, the tags still dangling. She began to set them down one by one. Each was white with lacy cups and silky straps "30D, 30DD, 32D, 32E" She said. "I want you to try each of these on. Once we find one that fits, we can get you the rest of the lingerie you need."

Audry poked at the top bra. "I'm going to need a lot of lingerie?" She asked doubtfully.

Jane got up and walked around the table. "If you're going to be my dream girl..." She grabbed the front of Audry's robe and pulled her up to her feet. "I like my presents wrapped." She pulled her into a deep kiss as her hand slid down to the robe's tie and she pulled it loose. The robe fell open.

Jane's hand traced up Audry's side and cupped her breast. Audry let out a sharp intake. She was still not used to the sensitivity of her nipples as Jane's thumb brushed against it.

"It's more fun to unwrap," Jane said and then continued to kiss Audry as she slid both hands up to Audry's shoulders and pushed the robe off allowing it to fall to the floor leaving Audry naked and vulnerable under the hands of this taller, stronger woman. She felt a growing wetness between her legs.

As though sensing Audry's excitement, Jane's hand

drifted down and her middle finger slipped up into Audry.

Audry's knees almost buckled at the alien sensation of having someone else, even a finger inside her. She let out a shuddering breath.

"See, being a woman can feel so good!" Jane whispered into Audry's ear just before she began to nibble it while her ring finger joined her middle finger inside Audry and began to slowly slide up and down against the front wall of her pussy.

Jane's tongue, lips and teeth against her ear sent waves of warm pulses through her head, down her neck, through her shoulders. Around her heart, the pulses met the electric tingles and surges she felt from Jane's stroking fingers.

"Oh GOD!" Audry moaned. She could not remember ever feeling this much pleasure as a man.

"Good Girl" Jane whispered, and the praise caused every sensation to intensify. "Come on" Jane said, she curled her fingers inside Audry to keep her grip and gently pulled as she walked backwards, Audry following, into the bedroom.

Jane's fingers left Audry and she almost let out a high pitched whine in protest but, before she could, Jane's wet middle finger slid up and found Audry's clit and began to rub. The high pitched whine still came out from deep in Audry's throat, but it was not one of protest. She felt the bed against the back of her legs and lowered herself down to it. Jane guided Audry down onto her back, smiled, licked her lips, and then, putting a hand on each of Audry's hips, she kissed Audry's pussy.

Jane's tongue did so much more than a finger ever could for Audry' clit and she let out a sound that could have been singing. The surge between her legs became a flood of sensation and the wave crashed over her. She curled her hands into fists. Her wrists bent in and her elbows flexed. The wave crashed again before the last one could recede and her feet, dangling off the edge of the bed, pointed down as her calf muscles contracted.

Jane was a master, licks, and suction and nibbles from her lips, she slid her hand up under her chin and inserted her fingers again.

The next wave crashed and Audry's breasts heaved as she gasped for air. She was drowning in her own orgasms "OoooowwwwwwoooooooooOAAAAA!!!!" She cried out.

Jane lifted her head, her chin shined. Her fingers continued their work as she looked down at Audrey. "This is just the beginning!" she said. She slid her finger out and left Audry gasping on the bed, wondering what just happened and how it was possible to feel like she had.

She heard Jane in the kitchen but didn't care much. She heard ice in a glass, she heard water run. She was thirsty too.

She heard glass tinkling as Jane returned. Something glass was in the drink she carried, a cylinder with a wide top sticking out of the water. "I brought some toys too!" Jane announced. A buzzing sound came alive and Audry could see a wand with a round bulbous head in her hand.

Audry's eyes went wide as Jane set the cup down beside the bed. Audry could see that the object in the ice water was a glass phallus, the sight puzzled and frightened her, then she felt Jane's fingers pulling at her labia, opening her before pressing the buzzing bulb up against her clit. Where before she had felt surges of pleasure with every lick and stroke, she now felt a constant and unending pulsing up into her belly, out her hips, down her legs, through all of her as the wand pressed and buzzed. Audry didn't make a sound, she was unable to as her mind folded in on itself under the ceaseless pleasure. She could feel the ocean rising once more and the waves would be greater still. Then Jane pressed a button, The one green light on the wand became two and the intensity grew beyond Audry's comprehension.

The wave rushed over her and she tensed and grunted through the pleasure. The next climax almost didn't wait for the first to end and her moaning grunt stretched into the third climax and rose again.

Jane pressed the button, a third light lit and the intensity exploded.

Audry ceased to be able to tell when one orgasm had ended before the next began. She was thumping the bed with her fists, her head and shoulders were off the bed. As she grunted she opened her mouth and a scream came flowing out!

She needed more, she needed something more, she needed something..inside.. “FUCK ME!” she cried out and she meant it. She wanted something inside her, she wanted to squeeze these new muscles around something.
Jane lowered the intensity to one light but kept the wand in place.
Audry laid back flat on the bed and gasped for air. She could still feel the pressure building toward orgasm, but the fact that she wasn’t having one at the moment seemed a merciful reprieve. Still, she needed that something more. Her eyes went to the cup on the nightstand and the glass cock in ice water. What would that feel like inside her? She needed to know. She looked back up at Jane pleading with her.
Jane smiled wide. “You want to be fucked girl?” Jane asked.
“Yes please” Audry said without hesitation or the slightest hint of masculine shame.
“Well, since you used the magic word.” Jane pulled the dripping glass dildo out of the water. It did not resemble any natural penis. It was more a work of abstract art. A round wide tip above a column of inter mixed ridges and ribs along the shaft before a wide flared base. “Is this what you want?”
Audry could feel the pressure toward orgasm inside her but it would not advance, she just felt like she teetered on the edge, she needed something more. She nodded.
Jane placed the tip against Audry’s opening, The

chill made her shiver. The cold seemed to intensify everything around it.

“Ready?” Jane asked.

“Fuck me! Please!” Audry begged.

The cold penetrated deep up into Audry’s belly, radiating out from the shaft inside her. Hard and inflexible, it absorbed the vibration of the wand and amplified it up inside Audry’s cunt and through what felt like her soul.

Jane’s merciless thumb pressed the arrow. Intensity increased as a second light lit up, thrumming deep inside her. !

Audry’s eyes rolled back as she was lost in absolute bliss.

Jane raised the intensity to 3 and then 4 lights!

The orgasms became constant and then indistinguishable, time melted away.

She saw John in the mirror and he turned to dust. She didn’t need him, or masculinity. That man’s life was not hers. She was Audry and she belonged to Jane who loved her, cared for her and brought her to this new state of being!

Her heart wanted to burst, her legs were shuddering, her abdominal muscles were beginning to cramp. The pain poked through the orgasmic rush washing through her.

“St-stoop” she gasped.

Immediately, the wand pulled away. One more orgasm ran through her and then the waves washed back leaving Audry bathed in sweat laying spent on the bed, her legs still shaking uncontrollably, each shudder sending another wave of sensation up through the glass dildo.

"Too much?" Jane asked.

Audry nodded.

Jane smiled and stroked Audry's wet hair out of her face, then bent down to kiss her.

As she did so, Audry could feel Jane pull the glass dildo out of her. She let out a sigh. She would miss that.

"We have the room all day." Jane whispered as she lay on the bed next to her. "Get some rest, then it's my turn."

Audry turned her head to look into Jane's eyes. She felt love, gratitude and an irresistible need to make her happy. "Yes my love"

6, Six Months Later

Audry sanded over the last peg-hole and brushed her thumb over the wood. A smooth unbroken surface, exactly what she wanted. Now all that was left was the wood stain. She stepped back and looked at her creation. Seamless smooth lines, ornate hand turned posts, sturdy, over-engineered and safe, with locking wheels and classic styling. The crib was the most beautiful thing she had ever made. As cliche as it sounded, perhaps love was the secret ingredient.

Audry corrected herself. The crib was the most beautiful thing she had ever made out of wood. The baby they had conceived in the elevator as John's last act of manhood would be the most beautiful thing she had ever created.

As she went over the wood with a wet cloth to remove any residual sawdust, Audry thought about what it would be like once the baby came. What being a mommy would entail. Two moms meant that, with the right amount of help, they could share the task of breastfeeding, though Audry clearly had the larger supply.

She looked at the project over one more time. Where water had yet to dry, the damp wood highlighted the grain. Audry had been meticulous in picking the right board for every single piece. Even those that would be covered by the mattress pad. The English walnut she had chosen would be ideal. The only downside would be the fumes.

"Now we need to teach your mom how to stain wood!" she said.

She felt a thump in response from her belly and smiled, rubbing her hand over the growing bump.

It seemed that Jane's ideal wife was one who bore all the babies and the potion had taken that literally. John may have released his sperm into Jane, but the magic had implanted the fertilized ovum in Audry somehow.

It was one last surprise from Mr. Raken's love potion 69.

Books By This Author

La Mascarade Du Café

Diagnosed with a terminal illness, Elle enters a world of dark desires at La Mascarade Du Café. Will she find life in surrender, or lose herself?

The Nexum Saga

In a near-future America, justice has been privatized, and punishment is property. Diana, wakes up to find herself at the epicenter of a corporate conspiracy, framed for crimes she didn't commit.

Rebalance Origin

The Gex plague wiped out most women. The Rebalance Initiative aims to save humanity, by turning unlucky men into breeding females. Clay is one of the first down this path.

Check Us Out!

Website: https://www.darkfantasymedia.com
Twitter: https://twitter.com/KatieOslow
Bluesky: @katieoslow.bsky.social

Made in the USA
Middletown, DE
06 May 2025

75167682R00146